The Mayfield Quick View Guide to the Internet for Students of Film and Theatre

Devi Snively
Central Washington University

Jeffrey Gress
Denison University

Jennifer Campbell Koella
University of Tennessee, Knoxville

Michael Keene
University of Tennessee, Knoxville

Mayfield Publishing Company
Mountain View, California
London • Toronto

International Standard Book Number 0-7674-1658-9

Manufactured in the United States of America
10   9   8   7   6   5   4   3   2   1

 This book is printed on recycled paper.

Mayfield Publishing Company
1280 Villa Street
Mountain View, California 94041

*The Internet addresses listed in the text were accurate at the time of publication.
The inclusion of a Web site does not indicate an endorsement by the authors or
Mayfield Publishing Company, and Mayfield does not guarantee the accuracy of
the information presented at these sites.*

CONTENTS

Chapter Four: Finding Internships and Jobs on the Internet 40
Sites to Search for Jobs 40
Creating Your Own Web Pages 41
Sending Your Résumé Electronically 43

Chapter Five: Internet Resources 44
Reference Material 44

Chapter Six: Film on the Internet 47
Introduction 47
Finding Out About Film Programs and Faculty 47
Online Discussions 48
World Wide Web Resources 50
Specific Areas of Film Studies 54
Future Directions 56
Cool Sites 56
Conclusion 56

Chapter Seven: Theatre on the Internet 58
Introduction 58
Overview of Resources 58
World Wide Web Resources 58

Theatre and Production Companies 60

Internet Glossary 66
Index 70

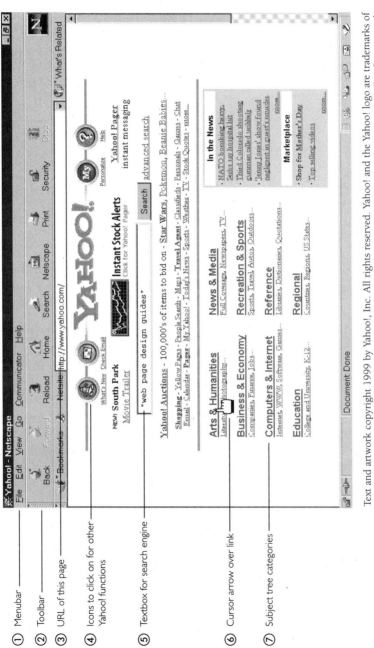

- ① Menubar
- ② Toolbar
- ③ URL of this page
- ④ Icons to click on for other Yahoo! functions
- ⑤ Textbox for search engine
- ⑥ Cursor arrow over link
- ⑦ Subject tree categories

INTRODUCTION

The dream behind the Web is of a common information space in which we can communicate by sharing information. Its universality is essential: the fact that a hypertext link can point to anything, be it personal, local, or global, be it draft or highly published.

> —Tim Berners-Lee, "Press FAQ." 7 December 1998
> <http://www.w3.org/People/Berners-Lee/FAQ.html>

What Can the Internet Do for You?

The **Internet** *is a vast resource*—not only for information, entertainment, and interaction with other people in other places who share your interests, but also for learning. You can do everything from reading newspapers and magazines to learning how to create your own Web page, to video-conferencing, to watching video clips from your favorite movies, to down-loading free software for your computer, to taking a virtual tour of Hawaii or Frank Lloyd Wright's house, Fallingwater. The Internet often has the most current news, the best views of the weather anywhere, the best maps, and up-to-the-minute discussions of current events. Additionally, it is convenient to have a variety of dictionaries, thesauruses, and encyclopedias on hand while writing a paper.

Beyond all those uses, *the Internet frees you from the physical boundaries of your hometown, your campus, your city, your state, and your country.* Information from Japan or Germany or Australia can come to you just as fast and easily as information from across the hall. Because the Internet does not have opening or closing hours, its information is more accessible than the information in your library. (And at many schools, more and more of the library's resources are available on the Internet.) Your school's library may be tiny, but with access to the Internet, you have more infor-mation at your fingertips than the biggest library anywhere. All you need to do is learn how to find it. To help you find information on the Internet quickly—and document it correctly—is the purpose of this book.

What Are the Internet and the World Wide Web?

The Internet is a global network of computers. It is composed of many parts, such as Web documents, e-mail, Telnet, file transfer, Usenet (newsgroups), and Gopher. Until the **World Wide Web** came along, the Internet was user hostile. *The Web is a huge number of sites of information within the Internet.*

Not only does the Web make accessing the Internet easier, but it also makes the Internet more fun because of the Web's **hypermedia** capabilities, such as audio, video, 3-D images, virtual reality, real-time communication, and animation. Sounds good, doesn't it? So let us help you get started!

QUICK VIEW:
How Can I Use Graphical Access to the Internet?

Many students have access to computers that already have Netscape, Explorer, or some other graphical browser. If that's your situation, this page will get you off to a fast start. If you need to start from scratch, go to page 5 for more detailed directions.

Using Netscape and Other Graphical Browsers

To access the Web's multimedia capabilities, you need a graphical **browser,** such as Netscape or Microsoft's Internet Explorer. (Note: You also need **TCP/IP** software; see page 5.) Netscape is used in the following description; other browsers, such as Explorer, work in essentially the same way.

Click on the Netscape icon to launch the program. The first Web **page** you see will depend on your **Internet service provider (ISP).** Most providers have designated a Web page to appear when you start Netscape. Many people like their first screen to be a search engine, such as Yahoo! <http://www.yahoo.com>. The Netscape Help button or the Yahoo! Help button will show you how to change your start-up page. (For more customization, see your browser's Preferences section, on the View menu.)

There are several ways to access a **Web page** using Netscape. One option is to follow a **hyperlink,** which can be either text or an image. Textual hyperlinks, or **hypertext,** have a different look from the rest of the text. Depending on the browser you use, hypertext will either be a different color or it will be underlined, or both. To follow a link, use your mouse to drag the arrow over the hypertext. When positioned over a link, the arrow will turn into a hand. Click the mouse, and you will go to that Web page. (Some links on some pages are not marked, but whenever your cursor arrow turns into a hand, you can click there and be taken somewhere else.)

Another option to clicking a link is to type out a page's address (called the **"uniform resource locator,"** or **URL).** Click on the Open button on the toolbar, type the URL in the box provided, and press Return. To navigate through a sequence of pages you have already seen, use the Back and Forward buttons on the toolbar. You may also access a Web page you have already seen by choosing it from your list of **Bookmarks,** from entries on the History list (from the Window menu), or from the Go menu.

(Note: All URLs in this book are enclosed in angle brackets, < >, for readability. The angle brackets are not part of the address.)

QUICK VIEW:
How Can I Use Text-Only Access to the Internet?

Some students have access to computers that will give them only text from the Internet. If your computer gives you access to Lynx or some other text-only browser, this page will help you get off to a fast start. Otherwise, please turn to page 5 for more detailed instructions.

Using Lynx and Other Text-Only Browsers

Lynx is the most popular text-only browser. With text-only browsers, you cannot view the multimedia functions on the Web, such as pictures, audio, or video. You see only text. (Note: You do not need TCP/IP software to use Lynx.)

If you have a computer account at school, find out if it is a **UNIX** or VMS account. Chances are it will be a UNIX account. (Lynx runs on both, but our example shows how it works on UNIX.) Next, find out whether Lynx is available; if so, you can access Lynx by logging on to your computer account and then on to Lynx. After logging on, you will see either a $ or a %. Then type `lynx`. Your screen will look like this:

```
$ lynx
```

The first screen displayed should be a page containing information about the World Wide Web and giving you access to other pages.

To access a specific Web page, type `lynx` followed by the specific Web page's Internet address (its URL). For example, if you wanted to go to Netscape's home page, your command line would look like this:

```
$ lynx http://www.home.netscape.com
```

When you view a Web page, the hypertext links (shortcuts to other pages) will appear in bold. To move your cursor to a link (in bold text), use your up and down arrow keys. When you place your cursor on the bold text, the text will become highlighted. To follow the link, press the right-arrow key. To go back, press the left-arrow key.

At the bottom of the screen, you will find a list of other commands. Simply type the first letter in the command name to execute that command. When you are finished, type `q` to quit. You will be asked if you really want to quit; type `y` for yes. This will bring you back to your system prompt (the $ or the %).

(Note: All URLs in this book are enclosed in angle brackets, < >, for readability. The angle brackets are not part of the address.)

CHAPTER ONE
FINDING INFORMATION ON THE INTERNET

The Internet started in the 1960s as a project by the U.S. government to link supercomputers; eventually, its networking technology also came to be used by academic institutions. In the beginning, the Internet was "user hostile," and the numbers of computers and people it connected were limited. With the creation of the World Wide Web in the early 1990s by Tim Berners-Lee in Switzerland, the Internet became much more "user friendly." Today, the Internet, a global network of computers, has a great many parts: the World Wide Web, Usenet, Gopher, Telnet, and FTP (file transfer protocol).

Technically, the World Wide Web is an Internet facility that uses hypertext to link multimedia sources. Web **servers** store files that can be viewed or downloaded with a Web **browser** via **HTTP** (hypertext transfer protocol). The most popular text-only browser is Lynx; some popular graphical browsers are Netscape, Explorer, and AOL (America On-Line). This book's examples use Netscape; Explorer works much the same way as Netscape.

How the Internet Works—In Brief

To find the information you want, you should know a little about how your computer works with the Internet. That is the subject of the next five brief sections. If you are not interested in learning more about how computers work, you can skip to "How to Find the Information You Want" on page 8.

Hardware and Software
To gain access to the Internet, you need a computer with the appropriate hardware and software and an Internet service provider (ISP). Some popular ISPs are AOL, Compuserve, MSN, and AT&T Worldnet. To access the Internet from home, you need a computer with a **modem** to connect your computer to the phone lines. Most modems run at 28.8K or 56K **bps** (**bits per second**). Faster modems can save you money if you are charged by the amount of time you spend on the Web. You will need a computer that has at least 16 megabytes (MB) of **RAM** (random-access memory). (Note: You will also need to find out the networking capabilities of your ISP; information is transferred only as fast as your ISP's slowest connection.)

For software, you will need TCP/IP (transmission control protocol/ Internet protocol, or languages that allow computers to communicate with each other) to provide an interface between your computer and the Internet. If you have a Macintosh, you need MacTCP. If you have an IBM or clone, you need Winsock (which stands for "Windows socket"). Generally these networking protocol utilities are already provided with your computer system. There are two main types of browsers, graphical and text-only, which were explained in more detail on pages 3 and 4.

Client/Server Systems

The Web works on a client/server system. The **client** is your computer and software; a server is any computer that houses files (text, audio, video, software) you want; and **networks** are systems that connect clients and servers. Think of your computer (the client) as a customer in a restaurant and the information provider (the server) as the chef. You order a meal (the information), and the waiter or waitress (the network) brings it back to you (your computer).

URLs and How They Work

To access a file by means of a Web browser, you must know the file's location. A URL (uniform resource locator), the Internet address for a file, is composed as follows:

```
protocol://server and domain name/file path/file
```

For example, suppose a student named Jane Smith at the University of Tennessee, Knoxville, has created a personal Web page for her résumé. The address for that page might be as follows:

```
http://funnelweb.utcc.utk.edu/~jSmith/Resume.html
```

Here, http is the **protocol**; funnelweb.utcc.utk.edu is the server and **domain name**; ~jSmith is the **file path**; and Resume.html is the file. When you type this address in Netscape or Lynx, the browser reads the URL's components to find the specific page. The first part of the URL not only tells you what type of file you are accessing, but it also tells the computer what kind of language it needs to speak. In this case, you want a Web page in **HTML** (hypertext mark-up language), so the computer needs to speak hypertext, using HTTP (hypertext transfer protocol).

The next thing your computer needs to know is where the file is kept. This is what the second part of the URL, the server and domain name, designates. The server where the Web page in this example is kept is called funnelweb. The funnelweb server is a computer at the University of Tennessee, Knoxville (UTK), that is denoted by utcc.utk.edu. The .edu tells you that the domain is "educational." Other types of domains are .com for "commercial"; .mil for "military"; .org for "organizational"; .net for "network"; and .gov for "governmental" sites. Recently, seven new domain categories were added: .firm for "business"; .store for "retail"; .nom for "individual"; .rec for "recreational"; .info for "informational"; .arts for "cultural"; and .web for "Web oriented" sites.

Of all the Web pages at UTK, how does your computer know which one is Jane Smith's? The last two parts of the URL tell how to get to Jane Smith's file. (Note the tilde symbol [~], which means that you are looking for a personal page.) The user identification for Jane's file path, or "user area," is ~jSmith. The file your computer wants is Resume.html. Now that the computer knows where to go, which file to get, and how to read it, the computer can display Jane Smith's page on your browser's screen (such as Netscape or Lynx). Notice that the file name has a mix of upper- and lowercase letters. Most URLs are case sensitive, so be sure to enter the URL exactly, including the uppercase letters. Note also that URLs never contain spaces.

Downloading Information

When you access a page, it sometimes takes a long time for the page to appear on your screen. If you are using Netscape and look at the bottom of the browser window while waiting for a Web page to appear, you should see a display indicating the percentage of the amount of data transferred. When you access a Web page, a copy of the file is transferred to your computer's memory. This is called **downloading** a file. So, when you are **surfing** the Web, copies of all those Web pages are downloaded to your computer. However, the file is not downloaded all at once; it is transferred in pieces, or **packets.** Depending on the size of the files you are downloading, the length of time it takes for the Web page to appear will vary: A large Web page or a Web page with lots of graphics will slow the transfer. Image files are larger than text files and take longer to download. To shorten the download time in Netscape, turn off Auto Load Images (from the Preferences menu under "View"). Also turn off **Java** loading. To remove the check mark, click on Auto Load Images. To turn Auto Load Images back on, simply click on that line and it will be reactivated. By turning off Images, Web pages containing graphics will download faster, but you will not see any of the graphics automatically. To see the graphics individually, you have to click on the picture frame; to see all the graphics at once, turn Auto Load Images back on and click on Reload (from the View menu) or on the Reload button on the toolbar. Your computer stores Web pages it has loaded in its **cache**; some computers empty their cache automatically, while with others you may need to empty it yourself.

Internet Service Providers (ISPs)

To get on to the Internet, you will need an Internet service provider (ISP). Before looking into commercial ISPs, check with your college or university's computing center because some schools offer Internet services for home access to students, faculty, and staff. Internet services through your school will probably be the best deal. Although your school may not always have the latest upgrades of hardware or software, the price will probably be hard to beat.

If you decide to go with a commercial ISP, you should do some comparison shopping. Think about what you will be using your Internet connection for, such as e-mail, Internet mail, graphical access to the Web, file transfer, Telnet, or storing Web pages. Once you decide what you will need, find out which ISPs offer all those services. After you have gathered a list of possible providers, ask some questions:

- What is the level of customer support, such as online help, user manuals, and telephone support (preferably 24 hours)?
- Is there an installation fee?
- Is there an extra cost for e-mail? If so, is the charge by message, by time, or by size of the message? Is there a storage fee for mail?
- Are there different rates for access at different times of the day?
- Is there a local dial-in number? Will long distance fees be charged?
- What is the **bandwidth** (the amount of information that can be transferred across a network at one time)? The size of the bandwidth can affect access speed.
- Is all the necessary software provided, such as TCP/IP and a browser (such as Netscape or Explorer)?
- Is storage space available for Web pages? If so, what is the charge?
- Are backup servers available to help maintain continuous access?
- What kind of security is offered?
- Read some reviews, such as those from *PC Week* (available on the Web).

How to Find the Information You Want

The Internet is a vast and rapidly changing conglomeration of information. Finding your way to the particular piece of information you need can be difficult if you are not familiar with the search options available.

World Wide Web Search Engines

You can search the Web with **search engines** such as Yahoo! or AltaVista; you can search FTP archives with **Archie** and **ArchiePlex**; you can burrow through **Gopher** with **Veronica**, Archie, **Jughead**, and Gopher Jewels; and you can access library computers directly with Hytelnet <http://www.lights.

A Note on the URLs in This Book

Change is inherent in the Web. As we prepared this guide, we verified every URL we list. But by the time you read this book, some of the URLs will almost certainly have changed. If you cannot find one of these URLs, try deleting the last set of letters in the URL (going "up" a level in the address). If that does not work, try searching for the page's title in your favorite search engine, such as Yahoo! or AltaVista.

com/hytelnet>. Sometimes the problem is *not finding enough information;* more often the problem is *finding way too much information;* and always the problem is *finding the right information.* Here are some suggestions for solving these problems.

Search engines are computer programs that allow you to find the information you want through key word searches. The search engine provides a text box, into which you type key words associated with the information you want. Most search engines also offer more complex searches involving some variation of **Boolean logic** with the aid of "logical operators," such as AND, OR, and NOT. (Some search engines let "+" stand for AND and "-" stand for NOT.) Some even offer more advanced searching, such as limiting your search to specific dates, ranking key words in order of appearance within the document, or giving you other ways to refine your search.

There are hundreds of search engines for the Internet—too many to discuss here. Two popular and different types of search engines, Yahoo! (a searchable, browsable directory) and AltaVista (a powerful search engine), are briefly described below. For a more extensive list of search engines, see the Library of Congress list at <http://lcweb.loc.gov/global/search.html>.

Yahoo! <http://www.yahoo.com>. Yahoo! is both a search engine and a directory made of subject trees. A **subject tree** is a hierarchical index system for finding information. You begin with a general subject, such as Medicine, and follow the subject tree's branches to a specific document. Yahoo!'s subject trees begin on its main page, which can be found at its URL.

Yahoo! is a good way to start searching because it looks at only a few key elements. Consequently, Yahoo! is the place to go for general discussions of your topic. To learn more about how to do a search on Yahoo!, click on the Options link located by the text box where you type in your key terms.

AltaVista <http://www.altavista.com>. Unlike Yahoo!, AltaVista does a thorough full-text search of documents for the key terms. If you put a fairly general key term into AltaVista, you will most likely receive hundreds or even thousands of links to pages that may only mention your topic in passing. AltaVista is a good place to search for obscure items or for very specific topics.

If you are getting too many hits for a topic on AltaVista, try doing the same search on Yahoo!; this should cut down the number of possible matches. Likewise, if you are searching on Yahoo! and you are not getting enough matches, try AltaVista.

AltaVista offers both a Simple Search and an Advanced Search. The Advanced Search helps you limit your results by specifying date ranges and ranking key terms. To find out more about Simple and Advanced Searches on AltaVista, click the Help button at the top of the first AltaVista page.

Metasearch engines. Today there are a number of metasearch engines— search engines that search a number of other search engines at one time. For example, on Dogpile (<http://www.dogpile.com>), instead of getting a result such as "15 hits found," you may read "5 hits on Yahoo!; 10 hits on AltaVista; 12 hits on InfoSeek," etc. Then you can choose which results you may want to look at. This feature is often a great timesaver. Interestingly, however, the same search that may turn up 15 hits on AltaVista if you use it through a metasearch engine, may also turn up 25 hits if you run it on AltaVista alone. As a consequence, while some people prefer metasearch engines, others (including this book's authors) prefer to use one or two or three separate search engines consistently. (Other metasearch engines are listed at <http://www.islandnet.com/~pb/frames.html>.)

Searching via Key Words
Key word searches may require some imagination if you are not getting the results you hoped for. In most cases, your search was either too narrow or too broad. The tips below should help. Also, when you do find information you want, remember to check it for credibility. (See pages 16–18 on how to judge the reliability of Internet information.)

Narrowing a search. If you are getting too many **hits** (successful key word matches), try narrowing your search by adding more key terms. Sometimes this will help, because most search engines will look for each of the terms independently but display the pages with the most matches first. Usually, you can narrow your search and make sure that all the key terms appear in the document by using AND between the key terms.

⌐🖰 ***Info Bit***—Narrow your search by looking for the most current information (or for the most relevant dates) in the AltaVista Advanced Search by entering a starting and an ending date for the information.

⌐⊟ *Info Bit*—Some search engines, such as Yahoo!, allow you to search within document titles only. This will narrow your search results and may give you better sources on your topic.

Broadening a search. If you are not getting enough hits, you need to broaden your search by deleting some of the more specific key terms or substituting synonyms for the key words you already have listed. For example, for a search about how to make a Web page, you might try several search strings, such as "Web page design," "creating a Web page," and "making a Web page." Also, you may want to try a more general category under which your topic falls. For example, if you want information on the Hopi god Kokopeli, but you get only one or two hits, you could try searching for "Hopi religion" or just "Hopi."

⌐⊟ *Info Bit*—The Web is a big place with millions of documents, and it is growing by the hour. No single search engine can cover the whole Web, because each search engine covers different, although overlapping, territory. If your search does not work with the first engine you use, try running it on several different ones, or try a metasearch engine.

⌐⊟ *Info Bit*—Some search engines are designed to find specific topics, such as Law Crawler at <http://www.lawcrawler.com> or the Amazing Environmental Organization Web Directory at <http://www. webdirectory.com>.

Finding phrases. If you want to find documents containing a specific phrase, such as "Green Bay Packers," put the phrase in double quotation marks to lock them together. Otherwise you will get thousands of pages that have only "green" or "bay" or "packers" in them.

Searching via Subject Trees

As described previously in the section on Yahoo!, a subject tree is a hierarchical index of topics that allows you to begin with a broad category and follow the subject tree's branches down to a specific file. Subject trees can be good places to start your search because you can get an idea of the different types of information available on your topic.

One of the first and best subject trees is The Virtual Library <http://www.w3.org/vl>. There are different ways to search The Virtual Library. You can start searching the Subject Index on the main page, or you can search the Category Subtree or the Top Ten Most Popular Fields.

Other Places to Start

You can start your Web research in many places besides search engines. One possibility is traditional reference tools (such as encyclopedias) that

Info Byte: Some Common Error Messages

Connection refused by server

Server is busy. The maximum number of simultaneous connections has probably been reached. Try again later.

Document contains no data

First, try clicking the link again. If this doesn't work, there may be a glitch in the network.

Forbidden access (Error 401)

For some reason, the creator or maintainer of a page does not want any "outside" visitors, and he or she has restricted the access to the page.

No DNS entry

Means "No Domain Name System," or that the server does not exist. If you are linking to a page from another, try clicking the link again. If you are entering the URL, make sure you have entered it correctly—with any capital letters and without spaces. If the URL is correct, the server may not be working.

Not found (Error 404)

The file you are looking for is not on this server. It may have been moved or deleted.

No response

There may be too many connections, or the server may be down for some reason. Try again later.

Transfer interrupted!

For some reason, the server was not able to transfer all of the data for this page. Try reloading.

Error 400

Your request could not be understood by the server. Your Web browser may be malfunctioning or your Internet connection may be unreliable. Try shutting down and restarting your computer.

are increasingly available on the Web. Some schools subscribe to such traditional reference tools so that their students can use them for free online. Otherwise, you can often find opportunities for limited-time free access to such valuable tools as *Encyclopedia Britiannica* (which often offers free trial subscriptions for a week at a time <http://www.eb.com>). Many teachers believe the best way to begin a research project is to consult such traditional reference tools; more and more of these are available on the Web.

Another possible place to start your Web research is to think about what kind of place might be likely to have information on your subject, and look for that place's Web site. For example, if you are researching a medical topic, why not start at the National Institutes of Health's home page (<http://www. nih.gov/>)? If you're writing about the FBI, you need to remember to look at the FBI's own site (<http://www.fbi.gov/>). If you're writing about any kind of historical topic, from the Dead Sea Scrolls to the Civil War, why not start at the Smithsonian (<http://www.si.edu/>)? Giving a few minutes' thought to what kind of place would be likely to have good information on your topic, and to finding and checking that place's Web site, can pay big dividends in research success. You can also try library search engines, especially the Library of Congress (<http://www.lcweb.loc.gov/>). (Be aware that library search engines often operate under a tighter set of search rules than Internet search engines, so if the key word you have chosen to use on a library search engine is not retrieving the kinds of sources you are looking for, you may need to try other key words or get help from a librarian.)

Other Protocols: Telnet and Gopher

Web servers communicate through HTTP (hypertext transfer protocol), but there are other, older information systems, such as Telnet and Gopher, that communicate through other protocols. The URLs for these other Internet systems begin with a different protocol abbreviation, or prompt, such as `ftp://`, `gopher://`, or `telnet://`. Telnet and Gopher are described here; FTP (file transfer protocol) is discussed in Chapter Three.

Telnet. Some electronic **bulletin boards,** library catalogs, and school computer accounts are not part of the Web. To access these sources, you need to use **Telnet,** a protocol that lets you communicate with computers that use the UNIX operating system. To use Telnet, you need to log on to another computer (a remote host). When you log on, a text-only screen identical to the screen of the remote host will appear. Then you can issue commands from your computer and have them carried out by the remote host.

A Telnet session's first screen usually lists instructions for logging on, accessing the Help page, and logging off. If you get a blank screen, try pressing Enter (or Return). If you get a screen with instructions, *read it carefully*, because when you want to exit a session, you may not remember how. If no instructions are given, try typing ? and pressing Enter to get the Help page. To exit, hold the Command key and type q if you are using a Macintosh, or hold the Control key and type q if you are using a PC.

To use Telnet, you will need Telnet software. If your ISP does not provide the software, you can download it from the Internet for free. For a Macintosh, get NCSA Telnet at <http://www.cstone.net/~rbraun/mac/telnet/>. For a PC, get EWAN Telnet from <http://www.iconn.iphil.net/services/telnet.html>. On the screen that appears, click on the Download button. Go to the bottom of the screen and type EWAN in the key word box and click on the Start Search button.

Gopher. Gopher is a menu-driven information system started at the University of Minnesota and named after its mascot, the "Gophers." It is a predecessor of the World Wide Web. However, Gopher menu systems and files can be accessed via the Web. There is a lot of good information on Gopher that is not available elswhere on the Internet. If you want to search Gopher, a good place to start is with Gopher Jewels at <http://www.uccs.edu/gopher/jewels.html>. Gopher Jewels catalogs many Gopher sites by subject tree. For a more thorough search of Gopher sites, use a search engine, such as Jughead (document title search) or Veronica (full-text search). For more on Gopher, Veronica, and Jughead, go to <http://lcweb.loc.gov/loc/guides/navigate.html>.

Integrating Research Sources
While the focus of this book is the World Wide Web, with particular attention to doing research on the Web and correctly citing your Web sources in your research papers, it needs to be pointed out that few college teachers today will accept papers that *only* use Web-based research, and some teachers frown on using *any* Web-based research. Thus, even if you are in a situation where Web research is acceptable, chances are you need to remember to integrate your Web research with information from traditional (print-based) sources as well. Here are two ways to go about integrating your research sources, accompanied by "road maps" to help you visualize each process.

Past-Present-Future (or General to Specific). A traditional approach to library research would suggest starting with reference tools (such as encyclopedias), moving on to books (by way of the Library of Congress subject headings list), then going to periodical publications (via periodical indexes). Finally, with a wealth of background information in hand, you could go on to collect firsthand information—from interviews, direct

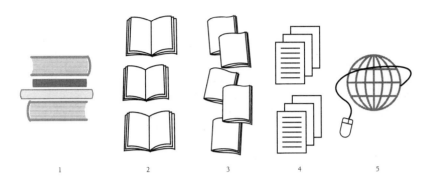

Road Map One: 1 = *reference tools;* 2 = *books;* 3 = *periodical articles;*
4 = *primary research;* 5 = *Web-based research*

observation, surveys, laboratory tests, or fieldwork. Within this structure,
the *last* step would be to do Web-based research, perhaps using as search
terms in Yahoo! and AltaVista the key words (including author's names)
gathered from all the earlier research steps. This method starts slowly but
hardly ever fails to produce rich results. The downside is that it starts so
slowly and the early stages are not much fun; consequently, some students
tend to put off starting until it really is too late for this rather deliberate
process to work. The upside is that given enough time and effort, the
process just about always works.

Start Hot, Finish Strong. Few people who become accustomed to
doing research on the Web can resist the temptation at least to try their
topic in a few search engines before they do anything else. Suppose you
are writing about "the role of sign language interpreters in the CIA"—why
not at least try that phrase, and a few variations of it, in your favorite
search engines before you do anything else? If you get some good hits, you
can still proceed backward through the previous pattern (roughly, Web
materials, then print periodical articles, then books, then reference tools,
then firsthand research), working from leads in Web-based sources
(authors' names, possible bibliographical information) through increasingly
broader (and, usually, older) sources.

Two cautions go with this method: First, if you do not find good Web
sources in the first step, you probably need to use the Past-Present-Future
method instead. Second, no matter how good the Web sources you may find
in the first step are, you *must still* do the other steps, and do them carefully

Road Map Two: 1 = Web-based research; 2 = periodical articles; 3 = books; 4 = reference sources; 5 = primary research

and thoroughly. Otherwise, you will risk writing a paper that is shallow and one-dimensional, and because you are relying too much on very few sources of only one kind, the tendency for accidental plagiarism is strong. The weak side of this process is that some students are tempted to stop after the first step. The strong side is that if you do get some good hits early on, that rush of initial success can carry you forward pretty far into the process.

How to Judge the Reliability of Internet Information

Students who are accustomed to doing research in libraries face new issues when they start doing research on the Internet. Before a book or journal appears in a university library, it has usually gone through a number of checks to make sure the information in it is reliable. For example, if you find a copy of *Moby Dick* in your university library, you can be sure you are getting a generally accepted version of the real thing. But if you find a copy of *Moby Dick* on the Internet, you need to give some thought to *where you found it,* whether the person who put it on the Internet is *a reliable authority on the subject* (someone who can be trusted not to enter his or her own personal, political, or scholarly biases into the text), and whether your professor will *accept your judgment* of the reliability of that material.

Arguably, student researchers should always make these decisions, even about materials they find in the university library. However, judging the reliability of sources found on the Internet is crucial because there is no regulating body that monitors the reliability of what is on the Internet. Although there is so much information on the Internet that it can seem like a university library, it is actually more like a huge open-air market. In one corner there might be reliable sources from whom you can obtain valuable information. But over in another corner there might be weirdos, whackos, and eccentrics, from whom anything you obtain is, at best, questionable. The problem is that on the Internet there is no way to tell the difference. Someone who wants to turn *Moby Dick* into a glorification of bloodsports or an animal rights tract can post a rewritten version with no indication of its differences from Melville's original. There's a saying in Latin, *caveat emptor*, or "let the buyer beware." When it comes to doing your research on the Internet, the saying should be *caveat internauta*, or "let the surfer beware."

Here is a list of points to consider when you are trying to judge the reliability of information you find on the Internet:

- **Who is the author or sponsor of the page?** On the page you are citing, or on a page linked to it, that individual or organization should be identified, that individual's qualifications should be apparent, and other avenues of verification should be open to you. For a good example of a reliable source, see "Notes about this document" for the hypertext version of *Pride and Prejudice* at <http://www.pemberley.com/janeinfo/ pridprej.html>. On the other hand, a page created by a person or an organization that does not provide this information is not a good source to cite. (You can often find out more about a page's source by deleting the last section of its URL and Reloading your browser, thus moving up a level in the Web site's hierarchy.)

- **Are there obvious reasons for bias?** If the page is presented by a tobacco company consortium, you should be suspicious of its reports on the addictiveness of nicotine. Is there any advertising? If the page is sponsored by Acme Track Shoes, you should be suspicious of its claims for Acme track shoes' performance.

- **Is contact information provided?** If the only identification available is something cryptic, such as "Society for Feruginous Retorts," be suspicious of the page's reliability. If the page is sponsored by a reputable person or organization, there should be some other way to verify that reputation, such as an e-mail or a postal address. (Note that a tilde [~] in the page's address usually indicates a personal home page and may require more searching for reliability.)

- **Is there a copyright symbol on the page?** If so, who holds the copyright?

- **Is this page a "zombie,"** or one considered "walking dead" because the person who posted it no longer maintains or updates it? Even though the information is "alive" in that it is still accessible, it is "dead" in that it could well be several years old!

- **What is the purpose of the page?** Why is this information being posted—as information, as a public service, as a news source, as a research tool for academics, as a personal ax to grind, or as a way to gain attention?

- **How well organized is the page?** Is the page easy to navigate? Is it complete? When was the page last updated? Is the information on it current? How credible are the links it provides?

- **Is the information on the page *primary* or *secondary*?** That is, is it a report of facts, such as a medical researcher's article counting cases of "mad cow" disease in England, thus making it primary information, or is it an Internet newsgroup discussion about "mad cow" disease, thus making it secondary information? The papers and reports you write for your college classes need to be based on primary information whenever possible. The further away from the primary sources your own sources are, the less reliable the information is.

- **Can you verify the information** on the Web page some other way? For example, can you check the page's bibliography (if there is one) against your library's holdings or check the information against a source in the library?

- **If you are worried that the information may lack credibility, try starting with a source you know is reputable.** For example, if you have to do a project on the latest in cancer research, you can begin your search at major cancer research institutes, such as Mayo Clinic in Rochester, Minnesota <http://www.mayo.edu>.

- Finally, remember that **even though a page might not meet your standards as a citable source, it may help you generate good ideas** or point to other usable sources. Also, be sure not to stop your search at the first page you find—shop around and do some comparing so that you can have points of reference.

Ultimately, the problem with reliability of information on the Web is like the whispering game children play. Someone whispers a message to the first child, who whispers it to the second, and so on. By the time it gets to the last child, the message is hopelessly distorted. Web pages can work the same way when people get their information from other people's Web pages: The first person who posts information may make a few small errors; the second unintentionally repeats them and makes one or two more; the third makes a few more; and so on. For information seekers it can be impossible to tell where in the chain the information is coming from, but that makes a difference in the information's reliability. So it is always a good idea to check against a library reference.

CHAPTER TWO
HOW TO DOCUMENT INFORMATION
FROM ELECTRONIC SOURCES

Whenever you are doing research and writing for a classroom assignment, documenting your sources correctly is important. If the information, ideas, or other kinds of materials (such as drawings and graphics) in your paper are from a source, you need to let your readers know by adding appropriate documentation. (And if you quote passages, you need to add quotation marks or make block quotations as well.) The documentation you provide needs to be complete enough that a reader who wants to check your sources will be able to find them. Material borrowed from the Internet and other electronic sources, just like print sources, must be properly documented. This chart compares the elements of documentation for print sources with those of documentation for electronic sources.

Books	Articles	Electronic Sources
Full name of author or editor	Full name of author	Full name of author (if available
Exact title	Exact title	Exact title
Place of publication	Journal name	Type of source (Web page, FTP site, online journal, CD-ROM, etc.)
	Volume and issue (if pages are numbered consecutively throughout the volume, you can omit issue number)	
Year of publication	Year of publication	Date accessed
Page numbers	Page numbers	URL (if appropriate)

Portable versus Online Sources

There are two kinds of electronic sources of information—*unchangeable* and *changeable*—and they need to be documented in slightly different ways.

Unchangeable (or Portable) Sources
Suppose you look up material on a **CD-ROM** (a compact disk with read-only memory), such as InfoTrac, Encarta, or some other portable database. As an electronic source, the CD-ROM is stable—that is, anyone could look at it today, next month, or next year, and find the same information. It has a date and place of publication (although here "publication" actually means "production") and a version number, which should be shown in your documentation just as they would be for a journal article. Thus, for unchangeable sources there is no need to add extra elements to your documentation.

Changeable (or Online) Sources
For materials you find on the Internet, you need to add some information to your documentation. Usually, it includes the date you accessed the information and its URL. Sometimes, you may be required to include the path you took to get to the page or even a hard copy (a printout) of the page. If information you find on the Internet is crucial to your work, it is always a good idea to print out a hard copy, just in case.

Different Styles for Different Fields

If you are taking a freshman or sophomore English or composition class, your teacher may require you to use the Modern Language Association (MLA) style, which is what literature and language specialists use. Or you may be given the choice of either MLA style or American Psychological Association (APA) style, which is what academics in the social sciences (such as psychology or education) generally use. When documenting Web and Internet sources, many teachers of first-year students recommend the Alliance for Computers and Writing (ACW) style <http://english.ttu.edu/acw>. Professors for higher-level classes or classes in other fields may expect you to use some other style—the Council of Biology Editors (CBE) style used in the life sciences; the *Chicago Manual of Style* (CMS) superscript style used in business, history, and many hard sciences; or even the Institute of Electrical and Electronic Engineers (IEEE) style <http://www.ieee.org> used in fields such as computer science. Although there are hundreds of different styles, the right one for you will probably look close to one of the four varieties presented here.

When and What to Document

Here are seven simple guidelines to help you decide when and what to document:

1. If you use the exact language of your source, you must use quotation marks and cite the source.

2. If you put the source's information into your own words (creating a paraphrase), you *still* must cite your source.

3. Use direct quotations only if there is something unique about your source's language or if your own words will not do the job better.

4. Directly quote only as much as you need—the bare minimum.

5. If you use information that is not common knowledge, you must cite the source. If this information would not be familiar to someone who had not researched the subject, it is not common knowledge and its source must be cited.

6. Cite all kinds of sources, not just words and facts. Sources can also include drawings, photos, artwork, ideas, music—anything you use that is not yours.

7. To work your quoted or otherwise borrowed material into the text more smoothly, introduce it with the name of the source. To introduce your borrowed material, use a tag line—for example, "As Dr. Stanley Prusiner, one of the leading authorities on prion diseases, said. . . ."

QUICK VIEW:
MODERN LANGUAGE ASSOCIATION (MLA) AUTHOR-PAGE STYLE

MLA style uses parenthetical citations within the text. They lead readers to a list of entries at the end of the document called *Works Cited*. Generally, the material within the parenthetical citation includes the author's name and the page number to which you are referring. Here we summarize briefly the MLA style of documentation, and on the next page we go into more detail about the MLA style for citing electronic sources. If you want more details about MLA documentation style, consult the *MLA Handbook for Writers of Research Papers*, 5th edition (1999). A basic MLA citation in the text will look like this:

```
...leads to better research (Morring 57).
```

This citation would lead readers to the following entry at the end of the document:

```
Morring, Frank, Jr. "Russian Hardware Allows
    Earlier Space Station Experiments." Aviation
    Week and Space Technology 16 (May 1994): 57.
```

Citations in the Text
In MLA style, parenthetical citations go at the end of the sentence in which the source material appears. If the sentence already includes the author's name, then only the page number appears in the parenthetical citation. In the case of more than one work by the same author, a short title is added in the parentheses. The page number is given in the parentheses, without *p.* or *pp.*

Parenthetical citations for direct quotations in the text appear after the closing quotation mark but before the final punctuation. Direct quotations that are more than four lines long should be indented an inch rather than enclosed in quotation marks. The parenthetical reference for such quotations follows the quotation's final punctuation.

Entries in the Works Cited List
The list of works cited includes only sources mentioned in the text and not all sources consulted. Entries are arranged alphabetically by the author's last name (or by the first significant word in the title if there is no author). The page is double spaced, with the first line of each entry flush left and subsequent lines indented half an inch (or five spaces on a typewriter). The basic pattern of an entry is author's name, title, and publication information (place, name of publisher, date, and page numbers).

MLA Style for Citing Electronic Sources

The MLA style for citing electronic sources is still evolving. Presented here is information from the current *MLA Handbook* (5th edition) as supplemented by MLA's Website <http://www.mla.org/main_stl.htm>.

CD-ROMs and Other Portable Databases

For unchangeable sources, the citation in the *Works Cited* list includes the author, title, and date information just as for print documents. After the title of the database, there is a period, followed by the producer's name and date of the product, if available. Finally, include the date you accessed the information.

> Morring, Frank, Jr. "Russian Hardware Allows
> Earlier Space Station Experiments." <u>Aviation
> Week and Space Technology</u> 16 (May 1994): 57.
> <u>InfoTrac: General Periodicals Index</u>. 10 Oct.
> 1998.

Online Sources

For changeable sources, use this format: author's name, full title (articles in quotation marks, books underlined) and any larger document of which it is a part, date of publication or most recent revision, date accessed, and the full URL address enclosed in angle brackets (< >). Here are two examples:

> Shepherdson, Charles. "History and the Real:
> Foucault with Lacan." <u>Postmodern Culture</u> 5.2
> (Jan. 1995). 15 May 1995 <http://jefferson.
> village.virginia.edu/pmc/shepherd.195.html>.
> Harnack, Andrew, and Gene Kleppinger. "Beyond the
> MLA Handbook: Documenting Electronic Sources on
> the Internet." <u>Kairos</u> 1.2 (1996). 10 Oct. 1996
> <http://english.ttu.edu/kairos/1.2>.

Ideally, the URL should not be interrupted by a line break; however, if it is too long to fit on one line, break the URL after a period or slash. The same form is used for a document retrieved from a file transfer protocol (FTP) archive, except the abbreviation ftp precedes the address, and the URL is not enclosed in angle brackets.

QUICK VIEW:
AMERICAN PSYCHOLOGICAL ASSOCIATION (APA)
AUTHOR-DATE STYLE

APA style places the author's name and date of publication within parentheses in the text, linked to a list of references (titled *References*) at the end of the document. Although the focus of this guide is electronic sources, here is a brief overview of APA documentation style. For more information, consult the *Publication Manual of the American Psychological Association*, 4th edition (1994).

Citations in the Text

Citations in the text generally include the author's last name and the year in parentheses. So a citation to something by Bill Jones in 1988 would be (Jones, 1988). The parenthetical citation precedes the sentence's final punctuation. If the author's name has already appeared in the sentence, the year of publication follows it in parentheses. APA requires page numbers only if you are citing a direct quotation or a specific table, figure, or equation. If you need to include page numbers (and some teachers want page numbers for everything), use *p.* or *pp.*

Parenthetical citations for direct quotations in the text appear after the closing quotation marks but before the final punctuation. If the quotation is more than forty words long, it should be indented an inch. If the quotation is set off, the citation appears after the quotation's final punctuation.

Entries in the References List

Each entry in the reference list must match a citation, and the entire list must be double spaced. The entries should be alphabetized by the author's last name and, in the case of multiple entries by one author, chronologically, beginning with the earliest. APA recommends that the first line of every entry should be flush left and subsequent lines indented. Each entry has four elements: author, date, title, and publication information. A typical entry for a book looks like this:

```
Schultz, E., & Lavenda, R. (1998) Cultural
    anthropology: Perspectives on the human
    condition (2nd ed.). Mountain View, CA:
    Mayfield.
```

Note: We show APA references here with "hanging" indents; some teachers may prefer paragraph-style indents (first line indented, subsequent lines at the margin). According to the FAQ on the APA Web site, either style may be acceptable.

APA Style for Citing Electronic Sources

The basic citation has five elements: author, date, title, document type, and publication information. The information here has been supplemented by APA's Web page, "How to Cite Information from the Internet and the World Wide Web" <http://www.apa.org/journals/webref.html>.

CD-ROMs and Other Portable Databases

If you use information from a CD-ROM or other unchangeable source (such as a magnetic tape or commercially produced disk), you need to name the author, date, and title just as for a print source. Next, specify the date accessed and the nature of the electronic medium. At the end of the entry, give the name and source location of the producer. A typical entry looks like this (because there is no author in this example, the publication's name comes first):

> The world factbook 1994. (1994). Washington, DC:
>
> Central Intelligence Agency. Retrieved Oct. 10,
>
> 1996, from CD-ROM.

You may encounter a CD-ROM version of a document that is also available in hard copy. If so, your citation needs to include information for both (while making it clear that you accessed the CD-ROM version). This note is for an abstract that was read on CD-ROM:

> Morring, F., Jr. (1994, May 16). Russian hardware
>
> allows earlier station experiments [Abstract].
>
> Aviation Week & Space Technology, 140, 57.
>
> Retrieved Oct. 10, 1996 from CD-ROM: InfoTrac
>
> General Periodicals Index-A: Abstract 15482317.

Online Sources

For changeable sources, use this format: author's name, date of the most recent revision (if available), title of the source, date of access, and identification of the type of document (such as online serial or personal home page). In place of a publisher is the complete URL. If the URL will not fit on one line, break it after a period or slash. Here is an example:

> Land, T. (1996, March 31). Web extension to
>
> American Psychological Association style
>
> (WEAPAS) [WWW document] (Rev. 1.2.4). URL
>
> retrieved April 24, 1997 from the World Wide
>
> Web: http://www.beadslands.com/weapas/.

QUICK VIEW:
CHICAGO MANUAL OF STYLE (CMS) SUPERSCRIPT SYSTEM

Three documentation systems are presented in *The Chicago Manual of Style,* 14th edition (1993). The one shown here uses superscript numbers keyed to numbered endnotes or footnotes. It is based on an adaptation of CMS style for college writers: *A Manual for Writers of Term Papers, Theses, and Dissertations,* 6th edition, by Kate Turabian (1996). In the FAQ on their Web page, the editors of *Chicago* recommend Turabian for writers whose manuscripts will *not* be published as books.

Citations in the Text
Note numbers that appear in the text are superscript numbers. They normally go at the end of the sentence, following the final punctuation; if they must be used within a sentence, they should go after a punctuation mark. CMS superscript notations in the text will look like this:

> One literary critic notes "Austen's uncertainty about the inner life of Darcy,"[1] and another explains that Austen's novels, like those of many other nineteenth-century British authors, empower their heroines "over their own plot" and place them at the center of the action.[2]

If you use a direct quotation in the text, the note number appears after the closing quotation mark. A direct quotation that is eight lines or more should be set off, single spaced, and indented four spaces. The note number appears right after the quotation's final punctuation.

Entries in the Notes List
Each entry in the list of notes should correspond to a superscript number in the text. The entries are arranged numerically, with the reference number followed by a period and a space. The entire list of notes should be double spaced, with the first line of each entry indented half an inch.

Each entry generally has four elements: author, title, publication information, and page numbers. The author's name is given in normal order (first name, then last name). Here is a basic entry for a book:

> 2. Hilary M. Lips, <u>Sex and Gender: An Introduction,</u> 3rd ed. (Mountain View, CA: Mayfield Publishing, 1997), 151.

If note number 3 were to that same source, just a different page, the entry would read

```
3. Ibid., 159.
```

CMS Style for Citing Electronic Sources

The CMS style for citing electronic sources is still evolving. The pattern for unchangeable sources presented here comes from the current (14th) edition. The pattern for changeable sources comes from the adaptation of CMS style by Kate Turabian (cited on the previous page). An excellent online source for more information about adapting CMS style for online documents is the CMS FAQ available at <http://www. press.uchicago.edu/ Misc/Chicago/cmosfaq.html>.

CD-ROMS and Other Portable Databases

For unchangeable electronic sources, the citation is like that for print sources, with the addition of the name of the producer or vendor and any access numbers associated with the document. Here is a sample entry:

```
1. Frank Morring, Jr., "Russian Hardware
Allows Earlier Station Experiments," Aviation Week
& Space Technology, 16 May 1994, 57; Abstract
15482317: InfoTrac General Periodicals Index-A
[CD-ROM], September 1996.
```

Online Sources

For changeable sources, the entry contains the usual elements for print sources, followed by an indication in square brackets of what type of document it is, the complete document address, and the date of access.

```
2. Charles Shepherdson, "History and the
Real: Foucault with Lacan," Postmodern Culture 5,
no. 2 (January 1995) [serial online]; available
from http://jefferson.village.virginia.edu/pmc/
shepherd.195.html; Internet; accessed 15 May 1995.
```

QUICK VIEW:
COUNCIL OF BIOLOGY EDITORS (CBE)
CITATION-SEQUENCE SYSTEM

The CBE style manual presents two systems of documentation. The one summarized here uses numbers in the text that refer to a numbered list of references at the end of the document. Because our purpose here is to show how CBE treats electronic sources, we summarize only the citation sequence system. For full details, refer to *Scientific Style and Format: The CBE Manual for Authors, Editors, and Publishers*, 6th edition (1994).

Citations in the Text
When a source is first used in the text, it is assigned a number that it retains whenever it is used again. The number appears in superscript immediately after the source is referred to, not separated by a space. If more than one source is cited, the numbers are separated by commas without spaces. Here is a typical entry (taken from *The Mayfield Handbook of Technical and Scientific Writing*):

> The oncogene <u>jun</u> has presently become one of the best-known oncogenes because of its ability to act as a transcription factor[1]. One study[2] examined . . . .

Entries in the References List
Titled *References* or *Cited References,* the whole list is double spaced. The sequence is established by the order in which the items appear in the text. The number of the entry is not indented and is followed by a period. Each entry has four basic elements: author, title, publication information, and page numbers. Authors' first and middle names are abbreviated, as are other elements, and the abbreviations are not followed by periods. Here is an example of a journal article entry:

> 1. Lenski RE, May RM. The evolution of virulence in parasites and pathogens: reconciliation between two competing hypotheses. J Theoret Biol 1994;169:253-65.

Here is a typical entry for a book:

> 13. Mandelbrot BB. The fractal geometry of nature. San Francisco: WH Freeman; 1995. 460 p.

CBE Style for Citing Electronic Sources

The CBE style for citing electronic sources is still evolving. The pattern for online sources recommended here is taken from *The Mayfield Handbook of Technical and Scientific Writing,* and is consistent with other CBE formats.

CD-ROMs and Other Portable Databases

For unchangeable sources, the author, date, and title information is provided just as for a print source. In brackets after the title, identify the medium. At the end of the entry, include the name of the database and its location. Here is a typical entry:

    9. Morring F Jr. Russian hardware allows earlier
       station experiments [CD-ROM]. Aviat Wk Space
       Technol 1994;140:57. Abstract from: InfoTrac
       General Periodicals Index-A: Abstract 15482317.

Online Sources

The *CBE Manual* does not require the full Internet address for changeable sources. Nonetheless, it makes sense to include this additional information. Here is a sample entry with the URL and date of access added:

    1. Brooker MIH, Slee AV. New taxa and some new
       nomenclature in *Eucalyptus*. Muelleria [abstract
       online] 1996; 9(75-85). Available from WWW;
       <http://155.187.10.12/cpbrpublications/
       brooker-slee2.html> (Accessed 1997 Feb 13).

Note that the type of online document is named and the date of access is provided.

CHAPTER THREE
COMMUNICATING ON THE INTERNET

Chapter One of this guide explained some of the most important ways people use the Internet to find information. The subject of this chapter is how to use the Internet to communicate with other people. Of course, making a distinction between these two activities is misleading. For example, when you join an e-mail listserv on the subject of technical communication <listserv@listserv.okstate.edu> because you want to learn more about the field and maybe find an internship, your primary motive may be communication, but you are certainly also finding information.

Communicating on the Internet takes many forms. Here is an overview of the topics discussed in this section:

- E-mail—How to send e-mail to your friends all over the world, how to read e-mail addresses, and how to use Internet mail.

- Netiquette—What you should and shouldn't do when you are communicating on the Internet.

- Discussion groups—How to subscribe to listserv mailing lists (and how to unsubscribe), how to take part in Usenet newsgroups.

- Real-time communication—What is Internet Relay Chat (IRC); what are MOOs, MUDs, MUSHs, and WOOs; what is videoconferencing?

- Electronic file transfer—An introduction to File Transfer Protocol (FTP) and how to do it.

- Risks and precautions—Find out what you need to know about computer security, disclosing personal information, copyright, libel, plagiarism, and viruses.

How to Communicate with E-Mail

E-mail is a way of sending messages electronically. If you get e-mail service through an ISP, you will be given a mailbox and software for reading and storing your mail, for composing and sending messages, and for creating mailing lists. There are lots of different e-mail software packages available, but they all work in much the same way. Most Web browsers such as Netscape and Explorer have built-in e-mail software.

When someone sends you a message, it will be temporarily stored on your ISP's mail server. You will use your e-mail software to see if you have any messages waiting. If you do, the e-mail software will download them from the mail server to your computer, where you can read, store, delete, reply to, print, or forward them.

When you get an e-mail account, you will be given an e-mail address. The address has three parts: for example, user_name@domain_name. Usually, you will be able to create your own user name, which is how your mailbox is identified. The at sign (@) separates the user name from the domain name. The domain name is the name of the computer or system where your e-mail is stored.

In the above e-mail address "user_name" and "domain_name" have no spaces (which is indicated by the underscore)—e-mail addresses cannot have any spaces. The address is also in all lowercase, because e-mail addresses are not case sensitive and are easier to read and type without caps. If you get mail returned because the address could not be found, make sure you have entered it correctly. If you have, and the mail is still returned, the person may have changed addresses or may be having problems with the mail system.

Internet Mail

Internet mail (e-mail sent over the Internet) takes e-mail a step further. For example, suppose you are surfing the Web and find a page that has great information, and you want to get in touch with the person who created the page. Usually, the person who created the page will include a link for sending e-mail. When you click the link, a window will appear where you can type and send a message. However, you need **SMTP** (Simple Mail Transfer Protocol) to send the message. Check with your ISP for the name of its SMTP server. To receive Internet e-mail, you will also need a **POP** (post office protocol) server. Check with your ISP for a list of services to see if POP mail accounts are available.

Virtual Communities: Listservs and Newsgroups

Virtual communities are ways of organizing or connecting people of like interests over the Internet. The following section discusses some modes of communication that are analogous to print newsletters.

Listserv Mailing Lists

Listservs are servers that house **mailing lists.** Listserv mailing lists are discussion groups categorized by special interest. Unlike Usenet newsgroups, which let you browse messages posted on Usenet (discussed next), listserv mail messages are sent directly to your e-mail address. When a member posts a message to the listserv, the message is delivered to every subscriber.

When you subscribe, your name and e-mail address are added to the mailing list. From that point on, you will receive all e-mail messages that

Info Byte: Netiquette

As with all human communities, even virtual ones, there is acceptable and unacceptable behavior. **Netiquette,** the guidelines for communicating with others on the Internet, helps us all respect the people who share our cyberspace. Most netiquette guidelines are just common sense, a reminder that even though we're in cyberspace, our relations with others are still human relations. Here are some tips:

- Do not use foul or abusive language.

- Do not force offensive material on unwilling participants.

- Do not join in **flaming** (by sending cruel e-mail to someone). Usually, flaming is started over not-so-commonsense breaches of netiquette.

- Do not shout (that is, do not use all caps) at other people on the Internet.

- Do not take off on tangents that are too far from a discussion group's stated purpose.

- Do not post ambiguous questions or ask questions that are answered in a group's Frequently Asked Questions (FAQ) list.

- Be careful to avoid **spamming,** or sending the same message (like a sales pitch) to many different addresses, especially listservs. Spamming is the equivalent of junk mail and will get you flamed in no time.

- Reread your Internet messages before sending them. Something written in haste may be misread.

- Lurk before you leap. (People who subscribe to a listserv and read its messages but do not post any of their own are said to be lurking.) Lurk for a couple of weeks and give yourself a chance to learn that virtual community's rules and temperament before you start posting. This precaution can protect you from making **newbie** mistakes and possibly getting flamed as a result.

are posted to the group. It is always wise to **lurk** (hang out and just read messages) for a while before joining the discussion. When you reply to an e-mail message from a listserv, you can mail the person who sent the message originally or you can post your response to the entire group.

One way to find a listserv for people with a particular interest is to do a key word search on a search engine, such as Yahoo! or AltaVista, by entering the topic and the word `listserv`. Or you can use the extensive mailing lists categorized by subject at "Liszt, the Mailing List Directory" <http://www.liszt.com>.

To subscribe to a list (list name and list address), send an e-mail message to the listserv address. Do not put anything in the subject line of the message. Then, on the first line of the body of the message, type the following:

SUB listname your full name

Once you subscribe, you will receive a set of instructions for list members. It will tell you where to post messages (usually a different address than the subscription address) and what subscription options you have (such as "digest," which combines each day's postings into one packet, or "unsubscribe"). Be sure to save this message!

To unsubscribe, send an e-mail message to the listserv subscription address. Again, do not put anything in the subject line of the message. Then, on the first line of the body of the message, type the following:

UNSUB listname your full name

Remember to unsubscribe if you terminate your e-mail account. Only you can unsubscribe your name from a list.

Usenet Newsgroups

Usenet is a computer network accessible on the Internet that is mainly used for discussion groups. **Newsgroups** are discussion groups on Usenet organized by interest categories. Newsgroups are essentially sets of archived messages, articles, or postings. You are free to browse any newsgroup's articles.

To access newsgroups, you need a newsreader. Most graphical browsers, such as Netscape and Explorer, come equipped with a newsreader. The next thing you need to know is the Network News Transfer Protocol (NNTP) server. Contact your ISP to find out the name of its NNTP server. Once you find out your NNTP server, you will need to adjust your Preferences setup. You will usually be given the choice to edit Mail and News Preferences, and you will find a space to add the name of the NNTP server. When you have finished, save your changes. You may have to restart your browser for the change to take effect. Now you can use the browser's newsreader to browse and respond to newsgroup discussions.

Newsgroups have many **threads** of discussion. A thread is the original message that begins a discussion and all of the replies to that message. Most browsers have options for following threads. For example, when you pull up a newsgroup article in Netscape, there are links at the top of the article to all of the messages in that thread.

Newsgroup articles can literally be here today and gone tomorrow. Because of the thousands of articles a newsgroup can receive in a day, old articles are deleted to make room for the new ones. Depending on how busy a newsgroup is, articles may be deleted within several hours. If you find an article you may want to refer to later, save or print a copy, because it may not be there the next time you look. To save a document as a file on your computer's hard drive, select Save from the File menu and choose a destination.

When accessing newsgroups, some of your basic options are to browse, read, or save newsgroup messages; to reply only to the person who posted a message or to the entire newsgroup; or to post a new message that starts a thread of discussion. Most newsreaders will have buttons for each of these options. As with listservs, it is a good idea to lurk on a newsgroup before you become an active member. To get an idea of what kinds of topics are appropriate, find out if the newsgroup has a **FAQ** (frequently asked questions) page. Newsgroup members will become irate if you post questions that are already discussed in the FAQ, and they will not appreciate messages that discuss topics beyond the scope of their newsgroup. If you make either of these mistakes, you could get flamed—bombarded with irate mail messages! (See Info Byte: Netiquette, page 32.)

Virtual Communities: Real-Time Communication

Real-time communication is different from the various forms of delayed communication that we have discussed so far—e-mail, listservs, and newsgroups. In real time, your messages—whether text, audio, or video—are seen almost instantaneously by those on your channel, instead of being sent and read later by the recipient. There are two main methods of real-time communication—chat groups via Internet Relay Chat (**IRC**) and multiuser domains (**MUDs, MOOs, MUSHs,** etc.).

To participate in real-time communication, you need some special software. Chat groups, MUDs, MOOs, and videoconferences each require different software; sometimes, different software is even required from chat room to chat room, from MUD to MUD, and so on. This section provides an overview of some of the real-time communication options, as well as links to some Web sites to help you get started. And remember, the same netiquette (see page 32) for other forms of communication is still in effect in real time. For example, avoid shouting (addressing people in all caps), and be careful not to divulge too much personal information.

Internet Relay Chat

Internet Relay Chat (IRC) is a protocol that gives you the ability to communicate in real time with people worldwide through **chat** groups. Once you have the proper software in place, you can connect to an IRC server. After you are connected to the server, you can sign on to one of the channels and communicate with others who are signed on to the same channel. You can have public conversation, where everyone on the channel is included, or a private conversation between you and one other person. Remember, though, that in IRC channels, the channel moderator can kick you off and refuse you future access, so follow netiquette (see page 32).

A good place to begin is with a document called The IRC Prelude, available at <http://www.irchelp.org/irchelp/>. Useful software that you can download is mIRC (a graphical client) at the address above, or LisztIRC at <www.liszt.com/chat/intro.html>. This page also provides IRC FAQs.

MUDs, MOOs, MUSHs, and WOOs

The first multiuser programming option was the Multiuser Domain (Dimension or Dungeon), or MUD. A MUD is a computer program that creates a world for users to log on to (usually by Telnet). Users can participate in role-playing, assuming various characters or personae. The next to come along were the MUD Object-Oriented environment, or MOO, and the Multiuser Shared Hallucination, or MUSH. MOOs, MUSHs, and other multiuser domains are similar. They all have a gathering of users, usually role-playing, but MOOs and MUSHs allow for physical objects to be placed in the virtual room where the participants are gathered. Among the latest in multiuser technology is the Web Object-Oriented environment, or **WOO**, where Web hypermedia capabilities are combined with MOO technology. These forms of real-time communication started out as ways of facilitating multiuser games. Now they are being used to create virtual societies. For beginner information, see the Megabyte University's Discussion List page at <http://www.daedalus.com/MBU/MBU.intro.html>. For more advanced information, see <www.csl.sony.co.jp/project/VS/index.html>.

A good place to get started with multiuser options is the Pueblo site at <http://www.chaco.com/pueblo/contents.html>. Pueblo is an example of client software needed to participate in virtual communities; this site also provides some general information and FAQs on multiuser communities.

Videoconferencing

Videoconferencing allows you and other people around the world who are signed on to the same conference, and who have the required audio and video software and hardware, to see and hear each other. You can also show each other images and text. One of the most popular software packages for videoconferencing is CU-SeeMe. For more information on videoconferencing, including CU-SeeMe and other software, go to "the cu-seeme cool site" at <http://rocketcharged.com/cu-seeme/>.

File Transfer Protocol (FTP)

File transfer protocol (FTP) allows you to send or retrieve files from one computer to another. In reference to the Internet, it usually means downloading files (such as text files and software programs) from the Internet to your computer. You can download huge amounts of software for free or for a minimal charge at FTP archives, such as Shareware.com at <http://www. shareware.com>.

To download a file from an FTP archive, you need to log in with a user name and password. Most FTP archives use anonymous FTP, meaning that you use the word "anonymous" as your user name and your e-mail address as your password. Browsers equipped with FTP software will do this automatically, so that when you click on a file you want to download, it will begin downloading immediately.

The Internet provides a vast number of downloadable files, such as HTML editors (used for creating Web pages), chat software, graphics animators, games (including virtual reality), and screen savers. The easiest way to find these files is to go directly to a file archive, such as Shareware.com, where you can do a key word search, search the New Arrivals, or browse Most Popular Selections (the most often downloaded selections). Much of the software is free, called **freeware**. Some software, called **shareware**, requires a small fee. (Don't let Shareware.com's name fool you; most of its software is free!) In addition to Shareware.com, a good place to find software (as well as reviews and ratings of software) is ZDNet at <http://www.zdnet.com>.

You can search for other FTP archives by using the search engine Archie, but Archie is not as user friendly as most of the search engines discussed so far. With Archie, you need to know the name of the software for which you are looking. There is also a Web-based interface for using Archie, called ArchiePlex. You can find a list of ArchiePlex servers at <http://cuiwww.unige.ch/archie.html>. Even though ArchiePlex is Web-based, it is still rather difficult to use, so read the instructions carefully before beginning any searches.

Most graphical Web browsers, such as Netscape and Explorer, come equipped with FTP software. However, this software is usually restricted to downloading files and is not capable of sending files. In order to send files, you need full-service FTP software, which you can download for free. For the Macintosh, you can get Fetch at <http://www.dartmouth.edu/pages/softdev/fetch.html>, or for a PC, you can get a free limited version of WS_FTP at <http://www.ipswitch.com/cgi/download_eval.pl?product=main>.

Risks and Precautions

The following section deals with some of the risks that you may encounter while working with the Internet. We also suggest some precautions that may help you avoid the most common pitfalls.

Privacy

It is not a good idea to put anything in an e-mail message that you would not want others to see, because messages can be intercepted or sent to the wrong person. Especially if the computer you are using (or your receiver is using) belongs to your school or employer, your messages are very easy for others to access. There are privacy programs available, but using such a program may make people suspect that something secret is going on.

If you turn your computer into a server, you can have problems with individuals being able to access documents and information on your machine other than what you want to publish.

Personal Security

Sometimes you may be asked to give personal information on the Internet, especially when downloading commercial software. Reputable businesses have taken precautions to ensure the security of the information you provide. However, if you are unsure of the vendor (or whenever you sign on to online news services), you should make a rule of giving just your first or last name and not giving your home address or phone number.

If you publish your own Web page (discussed in Chapter Four), be aware that your page is accessible to the public. You want to give careful consideration to the amount and kind of personal information that you post on your page, such as your picture, phone numbers, and addresses. It is one thing for the whole world to have your e-mail address; it may be quite another for the whole world to be able to recognize you on sight and drive to where you live.

Copyright

It is safe to assume that most of the material on the Internet is copyrighted. *The absence of a copyright notice does not mean that the material is not protected* or that it can be assumed to be in the public domain and therefore usable without seeking permission from the author or copyright holder. (For posting on the Web, however, the recommended procedure is to put "Copyright," the copyright symbol [©], the date published, the owner's name, and "All rights reserved" on documents that fall under copyright protection.) The only exception to using material from print sources that is protected by a copyright is "fair use," which usually means reproduction of a limited amount of material for educational purposes, criticism, comment, or news reporting. For more information on copyright issues, see <http://lcweb.loc.gov/copyright>.

Ideas, facts, titles, names, short phrases, and blank forms are not protected by copyright. Items in the public domain, such as government documents or items for which copyright has expired, are not protected by copyright and may be used without permission.

Libel
When someone knowingly spreads false information about another person, harming that person's reputation, or defaming them, it is called slander. However, when such information is published in print, it is defamatory writing and may be considered libelous. The same caution applies to writing published on the Web, so make sure that any information you post is true and verifiable. Libel is a crime and is punishable as a felony.

Plagiarism
For Web documents, you can create a link to someone's Web page, but *you may not* cut and paste any part of someone's Web page and place it on your own. Similarly, if you quote Web-page information in a written document, you must cite it properly. (See the section on documentation, starting on page 19.)

Viruses
Viruses can be devastating to your computer. They can damage or destroy both hardware and software. Viruses can get into your computer in several ways. One way is to put an infected disk into your computer's disk drive and open a file on it. Viruses can also be downloaded from the Internet when you transfer files to your computer—for example, by downloading software or text files. Viruses can also be sent via e-mail: Reading a message is not generally a problem, but if you open an attachment contaminated with a virus, your computer will become infected. Basically, if you do anything with e-mail beyond reading the message itself, your computer is susceptible to viruses.

You can use virus protection software to detect viruses and even prevent them from contaminating your computer. Some computers come with anti-virus software, but you can also purchase software or download it from the Internet. For the latest on computer viruses and anti-virus software, visit IBM's "Antivirus Online" at <http://www.av.ibm.com/current/FrontPage/>, the Federal Computer Incident Response Capability (FedCirc) site at <http://www.fedcirc.gov>, or the Department of Energy's Incident Advisory Capability site at <http://ciac.llnl.gov/>. At these sites, you will find information such as virus names, reviews of anti-virus software, and which viruses are currently at large.

Time Management

You can waste twenty-four hours a day, seven days a week, on the Web if you are not careful. A good practice, therefore, is to separate "fun" Web sessions from "work" Web sessions. Determine before you begin a Web session which kind of session you intend it to be and how much time you can give to it. Then stick to your plans.

CHAPTER FOUR
FINDING INTERNSHIPS AND JOBS
ON THE INTERNET

When you start looking for internships or jobs, the Internet has searchable databases of job postings by employers worldwide. This use of the Internet is one of its fastest-growing areas and one that is especially important for students. Depending on the position you are looking for, you can search by type of job, key word, or your skills, and by city, state, or country.

Sites to Search for Jobs

With services like The Career Search Launch Pad at <http://www.pantos.org/cslp>, you can access several job-search engines. The Web pages available from the Launch Pad are Career Mosaic, NationJob, Online Career Center, and Net Temps. You can access these career-search engines directly from the Launch Pad Web page, or you can link directly to each of them, using the URLs given below. Here are just a few of our favorite sites; you can find more on Mayfield's Web page at <http://www.mayfieldpub.com>.

America's Job Bank <http://www.ajb.dni.us/>

Career Mosaic <http://www.careermosaic.com>

Monster.Com <http://www.monster.com>

NationJob <http://www.nationjob.com>

Net Temps <http://www.net-temps.com>

✍ **Info Bit**—Many of the job-finding services allow you to post your own résumé in their databank, which can make it easier for employers who are looking for someone with your unique blend of education and experiences. Usually, for you to post your résumé you will need to have a version written in hypertext markup language (HTML). The section below (pages 41–43) on creating your own Web page will get you off to a good start in creating an HTML version of your résumé.

Internships
A great place to start looking for internships is Yahoo!'s Internships category at <http://dir.yahoo.com/Education/Career_and_Vocational/Career_Planning/Internships/>. Some other listings are as follows:

- Intern-Net
  http://www.InternshipPrograms.com/
- JobTrak
  http://beta.jobtrak.com/
- JobWeb
  http://www.jobweb.org
- Princeton Review
  http://www.review.com/career/find/intern.cfm

You can also find internships listed on the Web under particular fields (such as journalism) or particular locations (such as Washington, D.C.), or with particular companies (simply find your target employer's Web page and search it for an internships section).

Scholarships

To find scholarship opportunities, go to Yahoo!'s scholarship site at <http://search.yahoo.com/search?p=scholarships>. Another good list may be found at <http://sandburg.unm.edu/>.

Creating Your Own Web Pages

To post your own Web pages, you first need to make sure that your ISP has the ability to house them. There is usually an extra fee to store Web pages, so check to see what the rates are. Once you have a place to store your pages, the next step is to learn hypertext markup language (HTML). HTML uses tags contained in angle brackets, < >, to mark up the text of your document. Basically, HTML tags act as a set of instructions for the Web browser (such as Netscape); the tags tell the browser how your Web page should look (what's bold; what's in color; where pictures go), and how to respond to mouse clicks and keyboard strokes (if someone clicks on a link, where the browser should take them, or what Web page or file you are linking to). If you are not familiar with HTML, there is an excellent tutorial (created by Eric Meyer for Case Western University) called "Introduction to HTML." It can be found at <http://www.cwru.edu/help/introHTML/>. Also, after you start working with HTML, it's a good idea to have a cheat sheet with all the HTML tags. For such a list, go to the Bare Bones Guide for HTML 3.2 (or the most current version to date) by Kevin Werbach at <http://werbach.com/barebones/>.

Guidelines for Web page design. In many ways, good Web page design follows the same principles as good page design in general—the document should be professional in appearance, important design elements should be used in a consistent way, and the document should be easy for readers to use (you can find more on how these principles apply to print pages in *Easy Access,* Second Edition, by Michael Keene and Katherine Adams, Mayfield, 1999). Here's how these principles apply to Web pages:

- **The document should be professional in appearance.** Chiefly, this means the page should not be cluttered. Think of your screen as being divided into, at most, perhaps three blocks, with each block holding a different kind of element (text, links, visuals). Keeping background ("wallpaper") material to a minimum also helps keep the page uncluttered. The major sections of the document itself should be indicated by headings, lists should be separated from text, and any data should be displayed in simple tables. Adding a link to your e-mail address and a "last updated" date are good finishing touches for giving your page a professional appearance.

- **Important design elements should be used in a consistent way.** "White space"—areas of the page in which nothing is printed—is critical to the design of print publications, and at least equally critical to Web page design. The temptation for a newbie is to fill every pixel with colors and patterns. The logic, apparently, is, if there's any open space left at all, it's better to fill it with yet another dancing baby. But white space doesn't lie, and using lots of it in your Web page will really help the page's design. Use white space around the edges, at the tops and bottoms of screens, and especially between elements, whether vertical or horizontal. Instead of making long, endless pages, break them up into shorter, linked pages. Try to stick with just one or two typefaces throughout, rather than seeing how many different ones you can use.

- **The document should be easy for readers to use.** Keep each Web page short, and keep your pages up to date. Especially on the "front" pages, try to limit loading time by limiting visuals at least a little bit. When you do use images, try to keep the files small.

If you keep your Web pages uncluttered, use lots of white space, and make sure your pages load quickly, you're on your way to producing well-designed pages. Check your page on different machines and on different browsers to make sure that it looks the way you want it to. Also, remember that the information you are posting is available to anyone, so be careful what kind of personal information you post, such as pictures, phone numbers, and addresses (see Personal Security, page 37).

Once you have your Web pages ready for the rest of the world, the final step is to make them available through search engines (such as Yahoo! or AltaVista). For other people to be able to look up your page with a search engine, you have to submit it. Of course it would be quite time consuming to submit your page to each search engine. To help make this task easier, there is a free service called Submit It! at <http://www.submit-it.com>. Have fun!

Sending Your Résumé Electronically

If you have your résumé on the Web in HTML, obviously prospective employers can view it and download it or print it out as needed. If you do not have your résumé in that form, you may be asked to e-mail it to a prospective employer. In that case, here are a few pointers to remember: E-mail programs today do not handle things like different type fonts or sizes, boldface type, or italics; and fancy spacing (centering, lists that use hanging indents, etc.) usually just contributes to a document that comes out on the other end in a mess. If there is a chance you will need to e-mail your résumé, you need a very plain version—one in which all headings are at the left margin, only one type face is used (you can do some differentiation via uppercase letters, use asterisks instead of bullets, etc.), and, in general, all that fancy typography that makes your print or HTML résumé look so snazzy is gone. If you use a plain version, then your prospective employer just might get your résumé in an ungarbled form.

Putting your résumé into an attachment to a piece of e-mail is also not a good idea, because there's no guarantee at all that the person receiving that attachment has a program to open it that will be compatible with the program you used to create it. You're better off just to paste your résumé right into the body of your e-mail. Finally, remember that once you e-mail your résumé to someone, chances are that person is going to enter it into an electronic database that holds thousands of résumés, so that individuals within the company looking for new hires with particular qualifications can let their computers search the database for the key words that name those skills. What key words can be found on your résumé, and are they the right ones?

CHAPTER FIVE
INTERNET RESOURCES

Reference Material

Dictionaries and Thesauruses
- Bartlett's Quotations (1901 ed.)
  http://www.columbia.edu/acis/bartleby/bartlett
- Merriam Webster's Dictionary and Thesaurus
  http://www.m-w.com/home.htm
- Roget's Thesaurus (version 1.02)
  http://www.thesaurus.com
- Strunk's Elements of Style (1918 ed.)
  http://www.columbia.edu/acis/bartleby/strunk

See also the list at Yahoo!'s Dictionary List (under "Reference" on Yahoo!'s home page) or the list on Xplore's Reference section <http://www.xplore.com>.

Citations and Copyright
You can start with the copyright office at the Library of Congress <http://lcweb.loc.gov/copyright>, and then check "the copyright Web site" at <http://www.benedict.com>. There's a good discussion of citing sources at <http://libweb.sdsu.edu/cite.html>.

Libraries
- Library of Congress
  http://lcweb.loc.gov/library/
- Internet Public Library
  http://ipl.org

Newspapers
Nearly every large city newspaper has some kind of Web presence now. Some are only small bits of the print newspapers, and others require either registration, or subscription for money, or both, for you to access them. Besides the lists available on Yahoo!, there's a good geographic listing at <http://www.newsrack.com>.

Broadcast News
- CNN
  http://www.cnn.com
- National Public Radio
  http://www.npr.org
- PBS
  http://www.pbs.org

News Filters
Try the combination of **news filter** and screen saver at <http://www.pointcast.com>

Book Reviews
- BookWire
  http://www.bookwire.com
- The Independent Reader
  http://www.independentreader.com

Online Writing Centers
There's a comprehensive list of these wonderful facilities at the National Writing Centers Association's home page <http://departments.colgate.edu/diw/NWCA.html>.

People Finders
Most of the major search engines have people finders (as well as Postal Service address finders, e-mail address finders, and phone number finders) available from their home page. For example, you can find Yahoo!'s people finder at <http://people.yahoo.com>.

Image Finders
It is becoming easier and easier to find particular images (pictures, paintings, images of any kind) on the Web, with the help of such pages as Mister Pix, <http://www.mister-pix.com>, the AltaVista Photo Finder <http://image.altavista.com>, and the Yahoo! Image Surfer <http://ipix.yahoo.com>. If there is an image on the Web that you want to incorporate in a project, you can copy that image and save it to your computer. Once it is saved, you can put it on your Web page, put it in a word processing document, and the like. According to "fair use" guidelines, a limited amount of copyrighted material may be used without permission for educational purposes, criticism, comment, or news reporting.

Here's how to grab images from the Web. To save an image, place your mouse over the image. If you are using a PC, hold down a right-click. If you are using a Macintosh, hold down a regular click. You will be given a pop-up menu. From the menu, choose "Save Image As." You will be given a box with options for a file name (be sure to keep the same extension if you change the file name, e.g., **.gif** or **.jpg**) and a file location (to put it in the folder and drive of your choice). Once the file is saved, you can open the image in a graphics program, such as Adobe Photoshop or Super Paint. You can choose to "Copy" it. You can then place the image in a word processing document. Once it is copied, open your word processor to the file where you want the image placed, and "Paste" it. If you want to place the image in a Web page, then save the image to the appropriate folder, and reference the file in the HTML file.

Remember: You should assume that just about everything on the Web is protected by copyright. Material does not have to have a copyright symbol on it to be so protected. "Fair use" guidelines may be followed for use of copyrighted material without permission in student papers and projects.

CHAPTER SIX
FILM ON THE INTERNET
by Devi Snively

Introduction

Presumably you have read the previous chapters and now have a better understanding of the Internet, how it works and what it has to offer. Now what?

As a student of film, you can take advantage of the many resources on the Internet that are available to aid you specifically in your studies. So pick a search engine—any search engine, and enter the word "film." On Yahoo! alone, as of the writing of this guide, 10,244 sites matching this term were found.

For those of you with ample time and patience—go for it! For the rest of us, following are a few helpful hints to narrow down the otherwise daunting amount of resources available for film students browsing the net.

Finding Out About Film Programs and Faculty

In this day and age, most major colleges and universities provide information about their academic programs online in the form of home pages on the World Wide Web. These can be excellent resources from which to learn more about the focus of any given undergraduate or graduate program. These sites often include descriptions of specific courses and outline the interests and projects of each faculty member.

Many times, one can obtain the e-mail addresses of the faculty members as well. However, proceed with caution when doing so. Be concise and considerate when e-mailing a stranger—particularly one who may be in the position to give you a grade at some point!

Another benefit of visiting a school's Web page is that many will provide their requirements for admission as well as offer the opportunity to download an application right from your computer.

There are several ways to locate college and university Web sites:

If you are looking for information about a specific school, you need only to go to a search engine and punch in the appropriate key words (such as, Acme Film School) and chances are you will find what you are seeking.

If you are looking for programs in general, there are several sites that can be quite useful. Following are just a few of those options:

- Film schools (Provides links to film schools worldwide)
  http://www.filmmaker.com/school/
- Library of Annotated Film Schools, or LOAFS (A database of film schools' Web sites that also includes student reviews of different programs)
  http://www.filmmaker.com/loafs/
- Next Frame—UFVA Student Film and Video Festival School Directory (Provides a comprehensive list of online film/video/communication schools and programs available worldwide—categorized by country and by state)
  http://www.temple.edu/ufva/dirs/text52.html
- Yahoo! Movies (Offers a number of links to undergraduate and graduate programs and film-related workshops)
  http://asia.yahoo.com/entertainment/movies_and_film/film_schools/

Online Discussions

Usenet

If you find that class discussions are leaving you dissatisfied, another perk of using the Internet to broaden your film studies experience is the access to special interest discussion groups, or newsgroups as they are called. Usenet, which is short for Users' Network, is a UNIX-based information system that maintains thousands of these newsgroups, many of which are devoted entirely to film-related topics.

Usenet newsgroup discussions allow one to send and retrieve messages in a public forum. More often than not, there are no moderators to control the quantity or quality of messages, however. As a result, the discussions are highly unpredictable and can often get racy, heated, and downright offensive.

If you choose to avoid that degree of drama, you may prefer to participate in the moderated discussions in which at least one individual reads and judges the merits of messages before they are posted on the list. Moderated newsgroups frequently include the word "moderated" in their newsgroup name. Following are a few sites that offer more information about Usenet newsgroups and lists of current topics:

- Usenet Info. Center Launch Pad (A source for information on Usenet and its newsgroups)
  http://metalab.unc.edu/usenet-i/
- Dejanews (A guide to Usenet discussion groups)
  http://www.dejanews.com/

- Cyberfiber Newsgroups (A directory to Usenet and alt.com newgroups)
  http://www.cyberfiber.com/index.html

Listservs

Another option for discussion of a specific topic over the Internet is a listserv. Listservs are frequently moderated discussion groups distributed via e-mail from a central Internet server, called a listserver, that maintains a list of e-mail addresses of people involved in the discussion.

Listservs tend to be more exclusive as they are conducted among subscribers only. To join a listserv discussion you must subscribe by putting your name on a mailing list that copies and distributes electronic mail to all of the members. Once you subscribe, the subject matter is delivered regularly to your mailbox for you to read. Members of the group can post and read messages that are e-mailed to all involved. Members can respond to messages either publicly (on the list) or privately (through a direct e-mail message.)

Once you subscribe to a discussion group the listserver will automatically send you basic information about the group, including how to post messages and how to unsubscribe. It is generally wise to save that message.

A word of caution when subscribing to a listserv—research the list beforehand. Find out how many subscribers are involved. If you join a listserv with many subscribers, you may receive as many as hundreds of e-mails a day.

When seeking discussions about film, you may enter broad key words such as "film" or "cinema" for general discussions of those topics. If you are seeking information on a more specific area, you might choose to search for topics by director, film title, and so on. Following are a few sites that may help you to find listservs of interest:

- Findspot (A gateway to Internet search tools that includes a helpful listserv directory with other valuable Internet guides)
  http://www.findspot.com
- Publicly Accessible Mailing Lists (A guide to listservs arranged by subject and title)
  http://www.neosoft.com/internet/paml/
- Tile.Net/Lists (A directory of listservs categorized alphabetically)
  http://tile.net/lists/alphabeticalby.html

World Wide Web Resources

General Information and Links

With so many film resources on the Web, "index" home pages can serve as an excellent source for discovering sites of interest. Following is a list of some particularly helpful ones with respect to film studies:

- Cinemaniac (A database of film-related resources)
  http://frankmtsu.edu/~ipurcell/cinema/maincinema2.htm

- Cinemedia (A comprehensive directory of over 20,000 film-related sites)
  http://afi.cinemedia.org

- The Flying Inkpot's Incredible Movie Links Page (Guide to movie links on the Internet)
  http://www.inkpot.com/movielinks

- Internet Movie Database (Affiliated with amazon.com, this site offers free information of over 170,000 different movie titles.)
  http://www.imdb.com

- Screensite (A site that provides links to film and television resources with a focus on critical approaches to the media)
  http://www.tcf.ua.edu/screensite/

- Study of Film as Internet Application (or SOFIA) (Internet resources for film studies)
  http://homepages.unl.ac.uk/sofia/

Online Aids to Library Research

The Web is not limited to online resources. Many sites can also assist in the process of library research. Bibliographic databases, online catalogues, and descriptions of a wide variety of library materials can all be accessed online. The Internet cannot replace a trip to the library entirely, but it can certainly help you begin your research. Following are some online aids to get you started:

- American Film Institute (The Louis B. Mayer Library may be of particular interest.)
  http://www.afionline.org

- Bibliographical Aid for Film Research (The name pretty much says it all.)
  http://cwis.kub.nl/~fdl/general/people/western/findex.htm

- The Center for Motion Picture Study (Includes the Margaret Herrick Library and Archives)
  http://www.oscars.org

- Dogpile (This site checks dozens of search engines, news groups, newswires, etc. for information on any given topic you select via key words.)
http://www.dogpile.com
- Encyberpedia (Connects to online encyclopedias and similar resources)
http://www.encyberpedia.com
- Film Research & Resources (Theory and history tool for researchers)
http://www.gen.umn.edu/faculty_staff/yahnke
- 1stbookslibrary (Download more than 1,400 virtual books—many for free)
http://www.1stbooks.com
- Internet Public Library (Reference guide provided by University of Michigan)
http://www.ipl.org
- Library of Congress (Access to library's catalogs and texts)
http://lcweb.loc.gov
- Mediafinder (Provides information about 100,000 publications)
http://www.oxbridge.com
- Tisch Library: Film (Bibliography of print and electronic resources of film)
http://www.library.tufts.edu
- Virtual Reference Desk (Provides info on everything—including the kitchen sink)
http://www.refdesk.com
- Yearbook of Experts, Authorities and Spokespersons (Finds authorities on specific topic areas)
http://www.yearbooknews.com

Online Course Materials
Many faculty members at institutions around the world now post their syllabi, suggested reading lists, and other course-related materials on the Web. These references can be excellent ways to supplement your own coursework.

- Academic Information Film Studies (A database of film course-related materials)
http://academicinfo.net
- Films: Research and Resources (A site for students and educators to aid in film research put together by a professor at the University of Minnesota)
http://www.gen.umn.edu/faculty_staff/yahnke/film/default.htm

Film and Motion Picture Museums
Museum Web sites provide basic information about the museums and their collections, as well as offer helpful information and useful links to other relevant sources. Several even offer searchable databases of their collections.

- American Museum of the Moving Image (Brief page with basic information on this museum in Queens, New York, dedicated to the art and technology of motion pictures)
  http://www.ammi.org
- American WideScreen Museum (A cyber-museum dedicated to the history of widescreen cinema. Illustrated sections explain the history of cinerama and other widescreen formats.)
  http://simplecom.net/widefilm/widescreen/
- Berkeley Art Museum and Pacific Film Archive (Provides information about their film archives)
  http://www.bampfa.berkeley.edu
- The Bill Douglas Centre (Home page for center, which holds a large collection of early cinema books and materials)
  http://www.ex.ac.uk/billdouglas/contents.html/
- George Eastman House (International museum of photography and film)
  http://www.eastman.org
- Museum of Television & Radio (Homepage for the museum located in New York and Los Angeles that gives information about the collection, tours, events, and membership)
  http://www.mtr.org
- National Museum of Photography, Film and Television
  http://www.nmsiac.uk/nmpft

Professional Societies
An increasing number of professional societies have created Web pages to provide information about their organizations. Following are just a few examples of film organizations:

- Film Society of Lincoln Center (Offers information about membership, exhibits, and research)
  http://www.filmlinc.com
- Moving Image Society (Organization dedicated to all aspects of the study of the moving image)
  http://www.bsksts.com

- Society for Cinema Studies (Professional organization for educators, filmmakers, historians, critics, scholars, and others concerned with the study of the moving image)
  http://www.cinemastudies.org/
- University Film and Video Association (International organization for imagemakers, artists, teachers, and students)
  http://www.ufva.org

Journals and Online Publications
Many journals and publications have Web sites that post articles, offer indexes to current and past issues, and/or provide subscription and submission information. Following are some popular film-related journals worth checking out:

- Bright Lights Film Journal (Provides aesthetic and political examination of classic, commercial, and international film)
  http://www.brightlightsfilm.com
- Camera Obscura (Focuses on feminism, culture, and media studies)
  http://www.indiana.edu/~iupress/journals/cam.html
- Cineaste
  http://www.cineaste.com
- Film & History (A journal of film and television studies)
  http://www.h-net.msu.edu/~filmhis/
- Film & Television Studies
  http://English-server.hss.cmu.edu/filmtv/
- Film Historia (A trilingual journal dedicated to the study of the relationship between history and cinema studies)
  http://www.swcp/~cmora/historia.html
- Film Journal International
  http://www.filmjournal.com
- Film Quarterly (Berkeley Press's Publication covering the entire field of film studies)
  http://www-ucpress.berkeley.edu:80/journals/fq/index.html
- Images (A journal of film and pop culture)
  http://www.imagesjournal.com
- Journal of Cinema and Cultural Theory (Just as the name suggests)
  http://www.angelfire.com/ar/views/#ethno
- Kinema (Journal for film and audiovisual media)
  http://Arts.uwaterloo.ca/FINE/juhde/kinemahp.htm

- Kulture Void Pictures (Independent film Web journal)
  http://Kulture-void.com
- Macguffin (A film journal with Alfred Hitchcock focus)
  http://www.demon.co.uk/nscl/guff.html
- Millenium Film Journal (Examines independent/experimental and avante-garde film)
  http://www.h-net.msu.edu/~filmhis/
- Screen
  http://www.oup.co.uk/screen/scope
- 24 Frames per Second (Writing and reviews on films and filmmaking)
  http://www.24framespersecond.com

Specific Areas of Film Studies

As a student of film you may specialize in any number of areas. Whether it's film criticism, theory, history, or filmmaking, there are a number of resources dedicated solely to these categories.

Film Criticism

Film criticism on the Internet is highly variable. Sites can range from personal opinion-based movie reviews to more academically inclined theses on any given topic. The majority of these sites fall under personal home pages and should be used with caution with regard to the source. Many are simply entertainment-oriented. Those with more academic topics tend to be very specific, so it may be wise to use a film-themed database to find what you're looking for.

- Cinemachine (A movie review search engine)
  http://www.cinemachine.com
- Movie Reviews (Over 99,000 reviews by professional film critics of over 15,000 movie titles)
  http://www.mrqu.com/lookup?
- Mr. Cranky (An amusing, though highly commercial film review page that takes a purposefully cynical approach to film criticism)
  http://www.mrcranky.com

Film History

There are quite a few sites devoted to the study of film history. Remember to double-check your facts before relying on an unknown source, however.

- Classic Images (Information about obscure films and actors)
  http://www.classicimages.com

- Film and Movie History (Connects to film history pages)
  http://www.mediahistory.com/movies.html
- Encyclopedia Britannica Online (Has a reasonably large section on film history)
  http://Search.eb.com
- Film History
  http://www.cannylink.com
- Film History by Decade
  http://www.filmsite.org
- Technology and Society (Offers essays on the history of media in general with many specific pieces on cinema)
  http://www.cinemedia.net/sfcu-rmitannex/rnaughton/phd8400.html

Film Theory
At the time of writing there were surprisingly few sites devoted to Film Theory. Nonetheless, with the rapidly changing nature of the Internet that may no longer be the case. Some of the film databases mentioned earlier may be helpful in locating more sites and should be checked regularly.

- Auteur & Film Theory (Offers recommended reading lists)
  http://www.javari.com/auteur.html
- Film Theory Page
  http://Angelfire.com/al/icia/theory.html

Filmmaking
With the growing emergence of the independent film industry and the increased accessibility to filmmaking equipment, filmmakers no longer need to reside in Los Angeles to create their art. There are a vast number of resources available to filmmakers worldwide thanks to the Internet. Here are just a few of them:

- Annenberg/CPB Project Exhibits Collection (A brief introduction to the entire filmmaking process. Great for beginners)
  http://www.learner.org/exhibits/cinema/
- The Auteur Newsletter (Free online filmmakers newsletter)
  http://www.tk-productions.com/auteur/
- Cyber Film School (Toronto-based site offers articles, reviews, links, and discussion on filmmaking)
  http://www.cyberfilmschool.com

- Filmmakers FAQ (Offers answers to frequently asked questions about filmmaking)
  http://www.cinemagine-ltd.com/if-faq/frameset.html
- Film Underground (A resource for independent and underground film-makers)
  http://www.filmunderground.com/

Future Directions

Before long, Internet users will be able to watch entire feature-length films on their computers. Many sites already include animated images and audio and video recordings. With all of the rapid technological advances made on practically a daily basis, the resources available on the Internet are only likely to increase.

As a result, there will no doubt be more interactive resources, multimedia communication, and videoconferencing. This makes it all the more necessary to understand how the Internet works, how to take advantage of what is already out there, and how to stay current.

Cool Sites

Following are just a few examples of projects representative of the new media and new directions of interest to students of film that are offered by the Internet:

- Motion Picture Industry: Behind the Scenes (This site offers a variety of innovative options including a short student film and a blow-by-blow account of the making of the film. Takes forever to download, but impressive computer-generated special effects make it worthwhile. This site also has an interactive simulation that allows you to make your own virtual film.)
  http://Library.advanced.org/10015/
- Student Films (Watch student films or submit your own. Provides feedback and links)
  http://www.Studentfilms.com
- Trailer Park (Features new and classic movie trailers for viewing)
  http://www.movietrailers.com/

Conclusion

You've just read a very general overview of some options available to you for locating film resources on the Internet. With only a small amount of "surfing" you have likely become aware of how vast these options are. And this is only the beginning. This global network expands so rapidly on a daily basis that it would be nearly impossible to keep up. The World Wide Web has become a very valuable tool for exploring different types of media.

Nonetheless, the Internet is not without its flaws and setbacks. It is important to be aware of the problems as well as the benefits that it has to offer. The efficiency and power of your computer and modem will determine the access and speed at which you can utilize the resources on the Internet. This can lead to problems, particularly if your computer is outdated.

It is also difficult to determine the origins of much information on the Internet, making it nearly impossible to confirm the validity and accuracy of all of the information one finds there. This problem is usually resolved by supplementing Web surfing with more traditional methods of obtaining information, such as library research.

Finally, one must be sure to apply critical thinking and thoughtful analysis when evaluating different sources, taking into special consideration the inevitable biases, points of view, and authority that each member of the global community will have.

Once you've taken these things into careful consideration, enjoy! The Internet is an exciting mode of information, communication, entertainment, and education. With proper, responsible use, the possibilities the Internet offers are nearly endless—but one last word of caution . . . don't feel compelled to prove this theory. Fresh air, face-to-face human interaction, and books and films are still positive aspects of life that should not be overlooked. Always remember that your computer has a "Power Off" button, too!

CHAPTER SEVEN
THEATRE ON THE INTERNET
by Jeffrey Gress

Introduction

The following is a brief discussion of some of the many resources available to you on the World Wide Web. To take full advantage of these resources, first read and become familiar with how the Web is structured as detailed earlier in this book. You should be able to work with various search engines, listservs, news groups, and online Internet resources. Following is a listing by category that you can use to get started in your process of discovering the dizzying amount and diversity of information about the theatre on the World Wide Web.

Overview of Resources

As with any topic, you can begin your search by going to any of the search engines available on the Web. I often use the meta-engine Dogpile at <www.dogpile.com>. You could simply type in "Theatre" and see what happens. When I tried it, I received 2,537 hits, or individual sites, on the search engine GoTo.com, which is one of the many engines Dogpile surveys. Pages 8 and 9 of this book give you some tips on narrowing your search. For example, you might try "theater+technical+production+lighting" for which I received only 39 hits. I can then broaden or narrow my search based on those results.

I have broken the included sites into broad categories. First, I list some of the basic sites that offer a large selection of links of general interest. Then you will find sample listings of more specific content. Finally, I share some of the online "e-zines" and publications available. Be advised: Starting down any of these rabbit's holes may lead you to destinations unforeseen and rich in both entertainment *and* education.

World Wide Web Resources

Educational Organizations
- ATHE_NEWS/Association for Theatre in Higher Education (A listserv. To subscribe, send the message "sub ATHENEWS your name") listserv@lists.wayne.edu

- ATME On-Line (The Association of Theatre Movement Educators)
  http://www.asu.edu/cfa/atme/
- USITT (The United States Institute of Technology "is the association of design, production, and technology professionals in the performing arts and entertainment industry.")
  http://www.ffa.ucalgary.ca/usitt/

Theatre Training Programs
It seems that most colleges and universities have well-designed and informative Web pages that include introductions to their academic and extracurricular theatre programs. Here is a selection, ranging from relatively small liberal arts schools to large conservatories.

- The Intuitons College Theatre Guide (An extensive alphabetical listing American college and university theatre programs)
  http://dolphin.upenn.edu/~intuiton/guide/newguide.html
- Theatre Is Art (An even more complete alphabetical listing of programs)
  http://www.ram.org/notme/col_a.htm
- Department of Theatre at Briar Cliff College (A sample of a relatively simple and straightforward departmental homepage)
  http://www.briar-cliff.edu/theatre/index.htm
- Walnut Hills (An independent high school for the arts)
  http://www.walnuthillarts.org/HTML/welc4.html
- American Academy of Dramatic Arts (An internationally recognized professional actor training program. "This website presents some of the reasons for the Academy's success.")
  http://www.aada.org/
- College-Conservatory of Music at the University of Cincinnati (A noted conservatory training program)
  http://blues.fd1.uc.edu/www/ccm/

Internships are a popular way for students to gain real-world experience. Finding the right opportunity for you can be a challenge. The Web is an excellent way to get started on your search. Here are a few sites to start with.

- The Wooster Group ("The Wooster Group has played a pivotal role in bringing technically sophisticated and evocative uses of sound, film, and video into the realm of contemporary theater.")
  http://www.thewoostergroup.org/

- The American Conservatory Theatre (ACT is a Tony-award-winning regional theatre and training program.)
  http://www.act-sfbay.org/
- City Center NYC (One of the premier theatre and dance venues in New York)
  http://www.citytix.com/
- The Players of Sarasota (Sarasota's oldest performing arts company)
  http://www.sarasota-online.com/players/welcome.html

Theatre and Production Companies

Theatre and production companies fall into two broad categories: for-profit and not-for-profit. Here is a sample of each.

Nonprofit Theatres
- The Platteville Community Theatre Connection (Offers a terrific set of links to many of the country's theatres)
  http://www.daviestrek.com/pct/pctcnp.htm#Regional
- Acme Theatricks ("ACME Theatricks has been producing new work in Seattle for 10 years.")
  http://www.oz.net/~johnm/acmehome.html
- The American Repertory Theatre (Based in Cambridge, Massachusetts, ART is one of the leading regional theatres in the country.)
  http://www.amrep.org/
- Live Theatre Workshop (Proclaimed ". . . one of Tucson's most consistent and solidly entertaining small theater troupes")
  http://www.azstarnet.com/~ltw/
- Victory Gardens Theatre (A mission to support the work of Chicago-area playwrights has motivated this company since 1974.)
  http://www.victorygardens.org/b/index.html

For-Profit Production Companies
- Walt Disney World (What more can you say? Live entertainment producers for theme parks, ice shows, cruise ships, industrial entertainment, and business theatre)
  http://disney.go.com/DisneyWorld/index2.html
- Medieval Times ("Eat with your fingers and cheer on your battling Knight." Themed restaurants, parks, and nontraditional producers offer many entry-level and well-paying employment opportunities. Someone has to play the knight.)
  http://medievaltimes.com/index.htm

- Sandusky State Theatre (A typical producing theatre presenting a diverse mix of programming)
  http://www.state-theatre.com/

Commercial Theatre Sites

- CultureFinder.Com (Tickets and information about a wide variety of live performance events, organized by region or city)
  http://www.culturefinder.com/index.htm
- ESTA (Entertainment Services and Technology Association. An organization representing theatrical manufacturers, dealers, and vendors)
  http://www.esta.org/
- On Broadway ("A Site Dedicated to the Shows, Musicals, and History of the Great White Way")
  http://www.on-broadway.com/

General Information Sites

- Guide to Theatre Resources (A wide-ranging and terrific listing of both listservs and WWW sites. A little bit of everything)
  http://www-old.ircam.fr/divers/theatre-e.html
- McCoy's Guide (Self-described as "A Brief Guide to Internet Resources in Theatre and Performance Studies." All materials are copyrighted and are intended for use only in educational contexts.)
  http://www.stetson.edu/departments/csata/thr_guid.html
- Playbill (Commercial publication featuring a wide variety of free and subscription services as well as links to professional theatres and Theatre Central)
  http://www1.playbill.com/playbill/
- Showbits (An online shop for theatre gifts)
  http://showbits.com/
- Theatre Central (Provides links to all aspects of the theatre)
  http://www.playbill.com/cgi-bin/plb/central?cmd=start
- The Yale School of Drama (Information about this leading instruction institution as well as a great many theatre links)
  http://www.yale.edu/drama/
- WebRing.Org ("In each of its tens of thousands of rings, member web sites have banded together to form their sites into linked circles." The theatre section features a tremendous selection of amateur sites.)
  http://www.webring.org/ringworld/arts/theater.html

Specific Information Sites
Theatre History
- Mr. William Shakespeare and the Internet (Offers both a listing of information currently available on the Net and new materials specific to the site)
  http://daphne.palomar.edu/shakespeare/
- Restoration Drama Homepage (Presents comprehensive information about the Restoration Era in English Drama)
  http://ernie.bgsu.edu./~smorgan/publick/resthome.html

Playwrighting
- The Dramatic Exchange ("The Dramatic Exchange is a Web resource for playwrights, producers, and anybody interested in plays.")
  http://www.dramex.org/
- New Dramatists ("Called the 'Fort Knox of playwriting talent.'" Intended as a development workshop for emerging playwrights)
  http://fargo.itp.tsoa.nyu.edu/~diana/ndintro.html
- Playwrights on the Web ("A database of Playwrights and their Web sites")
  http://www.stageplays.com/writers.htm
- Screenwriters and Playwrights Home Page (Billed as "The Original Resource for Scriptwriters on the Internet")
  http://www.teleport.com/~cdeemer/scrwriter.html

Criticism
- Aisle Say—The Internet Magazine of Reviews and Opinion (Updated weekly, this primarily North American site deals with English-language theatre from around the world)
  http://www.escape.com/~theanet/AisleSay.html

Acting
- Acting Workshop On-Line (A comprehensive site for training, links, and professional information)
  http://www.execpc.com/~blankda/acting2.html
- The Improv Page ("A clearinghouse for information about improvisational theatre." Includes history, definitions, and many links)
  http://sunee.uwaterloo.ca/~broehl/improv/index.html

Design and Production
- ETEC (A full-service reference for all things related to technical production)
  http://www.etecnyc.net/

- Jules Fisher/Joshua Dachs Associates (Theatre planning and design; a leading theatre consultant firm)
  http://www.fda-online.com/
- Index of Knots and Lashings (Provided by the Australia Scouts, this comprehensive listing of rope work is a great resource for technicians and riggers.)
  http://www.scouts.asn.au/knot_idx.html
- Lighting Links Page (Presented by the Western Australia Academy of Performing Arts. A diverse listing of lighting-related information and links from around the world)
  http://waapa.cowan.edu.au/lx/

Theatre for Young Audiences
- Children's Theatre Resource Page ("The mission of this web page is to assist the growth of Children's Theatre into the 21st century. . . ." A listing of groups, resources, and links to assist producers)
  http://faculty-web.at.nwu.edu/theater/tya/

Management
- Americans for the Arts (A collection of advocacy and management information and links)
  http://www.artsusa.org/
- ArtsNet: Arts Management Information Service (A very diverse listing of management-related sites and organizations)
  http://artsnet.heinz.cmu.edu/
- The Foundation Center ("Your Gateway to Philanthropy on the World Wide Web." A site focused on assisting not-for-profits seeking funding and assistance)
  http://fdncenter.org/
- Fund Raiser Cyberzine (A guide to fund raising for not-for-profit arts organizations)
  http://www.fundsraiser.com/
- National Endowment for the Arts (A site serving as a gateway to the many resources available through this governmental organization.)
  http://arts.endow.gov/
- NAPAMA (The National Association of Professional Arts Managers and Agents, a national advocacy organization)
  http://www.napama.org/index.htm

- USAA (United Scenic Artists of America, the professional union representing theatrical and film designers and scenic artists)
  http://frontpage1.shadow.net/usa829fl/

A Sample of Individual Web Sites
- TECHnically Speaking (A a selection of general technical and specific biographical information compiled by "Dawn")
  http://www.scsn.net/users/ckeenan/dsunkle/theatre.html
- New York State Theatre Technical Information (A complete example of a state-of-the-art production facility)
  http://www-old.ircam.fr/divers/theatre-e.html

Research, Library, or Archival Sites
- ELAC Online Theatre Library (A wide variety of textual and historical resources as well as a variety of links)
  http://www.perspicacity.com/elactheatre/
- Gravel Walk to Theatre on the Net (An international site dedicated to assisting researchers in English and Swedish)
  http://www.ettnet.se/~pferm/gravel.htm
- The On-Line Books Page (A listing of books and links available for transfer)
  http://www.cs.cmu.edu/books.html
- UnCoverWeb ("A Current Awareness and Document Delivery Service." An index for print periodical and journal articles)
  http://uncweb.carl.org/
- The World Wide Web Virtual Library—Theatre and Drama (A collection of educational materials, scripts, and many links)
  http://www.brookes.ac.uk/VL/theatre/index.htm

Museums or Historically Significant Sites
- The Rebuilding of the Globe (The history of the original and the reconstruction project. Includes many terrific visual materials)
  http://www.clock.co.uk/face/features/0895/index.30.1.html

Publications
- On-Line Computer Library Center (Gives information about and links to thousands of libraries from all over the world)
  http://www.oclc.org/

- Theatre Education Literature Review (A diverse listing of Web-published articles)
  http://www.aaae.org/theatre/thfront.html
- Theatre Network Magazine (A cyberzine featuring many different theatre subjects. Offers calendars, reviews, and production materials)
  http://www.interlog.com/~artbiz/
- Theatre Perspectives International ("Intends to provide international theatre scholars and practitioners with an electronic journal devoted to history, theory, criticism, reviews and dramaturgy . . .")
  http://www.tesser.com/tpi/

INTERNET GLOSSARY

applet   See **Java**.

ASCII   The basic code e-mail uses; does not allow underlining, italics, etc.

Archie   A search engine for FTP archives.

ArchiePlex   Web-based interface for using Archie.

bandwidth   The amount of information that can be transferred across a network at one time.

bit   The smallest unit of information in a computer; represented by 0 or 1.

Boolean logic   A system for searching a database that uses the operators AND, OR, and NOT to look for two variables.

Bookmark   A tool provided by most Web browsers that enables you to save Web page URLs so that you can return to them at any time.

bps   A measure of data transmission capacity, used to describe a modem's speed, such as 28.8 Kbps (or 28,800 bits per second).

browser   An interface for reading information on the World Wide Web, either graphical (such as Netscape or Explorer) or textual (such as Lynx).

bulletin board (BBS)   Area where users can read and post messages as well as download files.

byte   A unit of information in a computer, equal to 8 bits.

cache   A region of memory where frequently accessed files can be stored for rapid retrieval.

CD-ROM (compact disk, read-only memory)   A compact disk used to store and retrieve computer data.

chat   Electronic conversations among Internet users taking place in real time in chat areas (or chat channels, groups, rooms, or sites).

client   The computer and software you use to access Internet servers.

DNS (domain name system)   The convention for translating the names of hosts into Internet address; see also **URL**.

domain name   The part of the Internet address (URL) that specifies the area on a computer reserved for a particular organization, such as mayfieldpub.com. In this example, .com stands for "commercial"; other types of organization designations include .edu for "educational" and .gov for "governmental."

download   To transfer information from one computer to another, or to transfer information from a network to your computer.

e-mail   Electronic mail, one of the most popular uses of the Internet, it can be sent to an individual or a list.

FAQ (frequently asked questions)   Lists of common questions about a particular product, service, or topic.

file path   Subdirectory in a URL, leading to the specific file you want.

flaming   Sending a large number of angry messages to someone who has usually broken the rules of netiquette.

freeware   Software you get for free.

FTP (file transfer protocol)   The standard protocol for transferring files across the Internet. Most browsers have one-way FTP; for two-way (the ability to send as well as receive), you can acquire FTP software for both Macintoshes (Fetch) and PCs (WS_FTP).

gateway   A device whose purpose is to aid in the transfer of packets of information from one network to another.

GIF (graphics interchange format)   File format for images that are viewable on the Web; see also **JPEG**.

Gopher   A menu-driven information system created at the University of Minnesota.

hits   The number of times a particular page is accessed, or the number of successful matches you receive during a key word search.

home page   The main, or starting, page for a series of Web pages.

HTML (hypertext markup language)   The formatting language of the World Wide Web.

HTTP (hypertext transfer protocol)   The protocol for reading HTML programs from the Web.

hyperlink   See **link**.

hypermedia   Links among various kinds of multimedia objects, such as video, audio, and virtual reality, in addition to text and graphics.

hypertext   A text link that takes you to another file on the Internet. A hypertext document contains hypertext or hyperlinks or both.

Internet   A global network of linked computers; home to the World Wide Web, newsgroups, bulletin boards, Gopher, and online forums.

IRC (Internet relay chat)   See **chat.**

ISP (Internet service provider)   A company that provides subscribers access to the Internet.

Java   Programmed mini-applications ("applets") for web browsers.

JPEG or **JPG** (joint photographic expert group)   File format for images that are viewable on the Web; see also GIF.

Jughead   A search engine for Gopher document titles.

link   Short for *hyperlink*. A link, textual or graphic, that takes you to another file on the Internet or another location in a document.

listserv   A program that distributes e-mail to a mailing list.

lurk   To browse and read messages, but not actively participate in a discussion group. A good idea before joining discussion groups.

mailing list   A discussion group that shares an interest in a particular topic; messages sent by members of the group are e-mailed to all its members.

modem   A device that allows a remote computer to communicate via phone lines to networks and other computers.

MOO (MUD object-oriented environment)   Multiple-user environment based on object-oriented programming technology. See **MUD.**

MUD (multiuser domain [dungeon or dimension])   Virtual environment on the Internet primarily used for role-playing games such as Dungeons and Dragons.

MUSH (multiuser shared hallucination)   A MUD variation.

netiquette   Etiquette on the Internet; the guidelines for preferred behavior when communicating with others on the Internet.

network   A system of computers that can transmit information from one to another.

newbie   Someone new to the Web.

news filter   A software program that lets you customize your news. You can choose what type of news you want and from what source.

newsgroup   A discussion group, or informal bulletin board, that shares an interest in a particular topic; newsgroups are located on Usenet, where articles are read and posted.

packet   When information is transferred from the Internet to your computer, it is broken into pieces, or packets, which are transmitted to your computer and reassembled by TCP software.

page   Any Web document viewable with a browser.

platform   The operating system that your computer runs—for example, DOS (disk operating system), Windows, or Macintosh.

POP (post office protocol)   The standard protocol for reading Internet mail sent using SMTP.

portal   A Web page that combines search engine, subject tree, newsfilter, etc. Most major search engines now have first pages that are actually portals.

protocol   Information format. The protocol lets two computers know what type of information is being transferred. The protocol for transferring information across the Internet is given in the first part of the URL (e.g., http, ftp, gopher, telnet).

RAM (random access memory)   The amount of available short-term memory in a computer directly correlating to the speed of your processor—the more RAM you have, the faster your computer is.

real-time communication   Communication in which your messages are seen instantly; makes possible "live" conversations.

ROM (read-only memory)   The unchangeable portion of the computer's memory containing the start-up instructions for your system.

route   The path a packet takes from the server to the client.

search engine   A program that allows you to perform keyword searches to locate Web documents.

server   A computer accessible to other networked computers.

shareware   Copyrighted software that is distributed on a trial basis; you eventually have to pay for it if you want to continue to use it beyond the trial period. The cost is generally minimal.

SMTP (simple mail transfer protocol)   The standard protocol for transferring e-mail from one computer to another across the Internet.

spam   Unsolicited e-mail usually sent to a large number of users, such as to a Usenet group or a listserv mailing list.

subject tree   A hierarchical directory of information.

surfing   Aimlessly exploring the Internet by clicking links from one page to another.

tags   Codes used in hypertext markup language (HTML).

TCP/IP (transmission control protocol/Internet protocol)   TCP is the software your computer uses to create an interface with the Internet. TCP software receives the packets of data transmitted across the Internet and reassembles the corresponding file so that you can view the resulting Web page. IP is the protocol that computers use to talk to each other on the Internet, and it helps to define the route packets take.

Telnet   A standard protocol for logging on to another computer remotely. For example, if you want to log on from home to your UNIX account at school, you can use Telnet.

thread   The original newsgroup message (article) and all of its associated replies.

UNIX   A freeware computer operating system used by many colleges and universities.

URL (uniform resource locator)   An address for an Internet location.

Usenet   A UNIX-based computing system used mainly for discussion and newsgroups.

Veronica   A program that searches the full text of Gopher documents.

videoconference   Two or more people interacting through real-time video and audio feeds.

virus   A self-replicating destructive program that can be downloaded from the Internet or obtained via an infected file on a diskette. A few viruses are harmless and even amusing, but most can destroy the data on your hard disk.

Web page   A document accessible on the Web.

World Wide Web   The segment of the Internet that uses primarily HTTP.

WOO (Web object-oriented environment)   A virtual space primarily used for role-playing similar to MUD, but located on the World Wide Web.

INDEX

Academic Information Film Studies, 51

Acme Theatricks (Seattle), 60

Acting Workshop On-Line, 62

Adams, Katherine, 42

addresses
e-mail, 31
subscription, 33
URL, 3, 4, 6–7, 9, 23, 69

Aisle Say, 62

Alliance for Computers and Writing (ACW), 20

AltaVista, 8, 9–10, 32, 43

American Academy of Dramatic Arts, 59

American Conservatory Theatre (ACT), 59

American Film Institute, 50

American Museum of the Moving Image, 52

American Psychological Association (APA), 20, 24–25

American Repertory Theatre (ART), 60

American WideScreen Museum, 52

Americans for the Arts, 63

angle brackets, 3, 4, 23, 41

Annenberg/CPB Project Exhibits Collection, 55

anti-virus software, 38–39

AOL (America On-Line), 5

Archie, 8, 36, 66

ArchiePlex, 8, 36, 66

ArtsNet: Arts Management Information Service, 63

ASCII, 66

Association of Theatre Movement Educators, 58

at (@) sign, 31

AT&T Worldnet, 5

ATHE_NEWS/Association for Theatre in Higher Education, 58

ATME On-Line, 58

attached files, 43

Auteur & Film Theory, 55

Auteur Newsletter, 55

Auto Load Images, 7

bandwidth, 8, 66

Berkeley Art Museum and Pacific Film Archive, 52

Berners-Lee, Tim, 1, 5

bias, 17

Bibliographical Aid for Film Research, 50

Bill Douglas Centre, 52

bit, 5, 66

block quotations, 19

book(s) and book reviews, 45

Bookmarks, 3, 66

Boolean logic, 9, 66

bps (bits per second), 5, 66

Briar Cliff College Department of Theatre, 59

Bright Lights Film Journal, 53

broadcast news, 45

browsers
defined, 66
e-mail software on, 30
FTP software on, 36
graphical, 3, 5, 6
options for following threads, 33
preferences section of, 3, 7
text-only, 4, 5, 6
using, 3
See also specific browsers

bulletin board (BBS), 13, 66

byte, 66

cache, 7, 66

Camera Obscura, 53

career-search engines, 40

case sensitivity, 7

CD-ROM, 23, 25, 27, 29, 66

Center for Motion Picture Study, 50

On-Line Computer Library Center, 64
online sources, 19–20, 23, 25, 27, 29.
    See also research sources

packets, 7, 68
page, 68. *See also* Web pages
paraphrasing, 21
parenthetical citations, 22, 24
PC (personal computer) software, 5–6,
    14, 36
people finders, 45
personal information, 37, 42
plagiarism, 38
platform, 68
Platteville Community Theatre
    Connection, 60
Playbill, 61
Players of Sarasota, 60
playwrighting Web sites, 62
Playwrights on the Web, 62
POP (post office protocol), 31, 68
portable sources, 19–20, 23, 25, 27,
    29
portal, 68
preferences, 3, 7
privacy, 37
production
    film, 60
    theatrical, 62–63
professional societies, 52–53
prompt, 4
protocols, 5, 6, 13–14, 31, 68
publications
    about film, 53–54
    about theatre, 64–65
Publicly Accessible Mailing Lists, 49

question mark, 14
quotation marks, 11, 19, 20

RAM (random-access memory), 5, 68
real-time communication, 34–35, 68
Rebuilding of the Globe, 64
reference tools, 11, 13, 14–16, 44–45
reliability, 16–18
research sources, 44–46

changeable (online), 19, 20, 23, 25,
    27, 29
    documenting, 19–29
    for film, 50–51
    integrating, 14–16
    for theatre, 64
    unchangeable (portable), 19–20, 23,
        25, 27, 29
Restoration Drama Homepage, 62
résumés, 43
ROM (read-only memory), 68
route, 68

Sandusky State Theatre, 60
scholarships, 41
schools
    for film studies, 47–48
    for theatrical studies, 58–59
screen savers, 36
Screensite, 50
Screenwriters and Playwrights Home
    Page, 62
search(es)
    Boolean, 9, 66
    broadening, 11
    job, 40, 43
    key word, 10–11
    narrowing, 10–11
    via subject trees, 9, 11
    traditional reference tools for, 11,
        13, 14–15
search engines, 3, 8–10, 11, 36, 40, 43,
    69
security, 37, 42
servers, 5, 6, 12, 69
shareware, 36, 69
Showbits, 61
SMTP (Simple Mail Transfer Protocol),
    31, 69
Society for Cinema Studies, 53
SOFIA (Study of Film as Internet
    Application), 50
software, 5–6, 14, 36, 38–39
    anti-virus, 38–39
    e-mail, 30–31
    freeware, 36, 67

FAVORITE WEB SITES

Name of Site: _____

URL: _____

Name of Site: _____

URL: _____

Name of Site: _____

URL: _____

Name of Site: _____

URL: _____

Name of Site: _____

URL: _____

Name of Site: _____

URL: _____

Name of Site: _____

URL: _____

Name of Site: _____

URL: _____

Name of Site: _____

URL: _____

Name of Site: _____

URL: _____

Name of Site: _____

URL: _____

Name of Site: _____

URL: _____

Name of Site: _____

URL: _____

Name of Site: _____

URL: _____

Name of Site: _____

URL: _____

Name of Site: _____

URL: _____

Name of Site: _____

URL: _____

Name of Site: _____

URL: _____

Name of Site: _____

URL: _____

Name of Site: _____

URL: _____

Name of Site: _____

URL: _____

Name of Site: _____

URL: _____

Name of Site: _____

URL: _____

Name of Site: _____

URL: _____

Name of Site: _____

URL: _____

Name of Site: _____

URL: _____

Name of Site: _____

URL: _____

Name of Site: _____

URL: _____

Name of Site: _____

URL: _____

Name of Site: _____

URL: _____

Name of Site: _____

URL: _____

Name of Site: _____

URL: _____

Name of Site: _____

URL: _____

Name of Site: _____

URL: _____

Name of Site: _____

URL: _____

Name of Site: _____

URL: _____

Name of Site: _____

URL: _____

Name of Site: _____

URL: _____

Name of Site: _____

URL: _____

Name of Site: _____

URL: _____

Name of Site: _____

URL: _____

Name of Site: _____

URL: _____

Name of Site: _____

URL: _____

Name of Site: _____

URL: _____

Name of Site: _____

URL: _____

Name of Site: _____

URL: _____

Name of Site: _____

URL: _____

Name of Site: _____

URL: _____

Name of Site: _____

URL: _____

Name of Site: _____

URL: _____

Name of Site: _____

URL: _____

Name of Site: _____

URL: _____

Name of Site: _____

URL: _____

Name of Site: _____

URL: _____

Name of Site: _____

URL: _____

Name of Site: _____

URL: _____

Name of Site: _____

URL: _____

Name of Site: _____

URL: _____

Name of Site: _____

URL: _____

Name of Site: _____

URL: _____

Name of Site: _____

URL: _____

Name of Site: _____

URL: _____

Name of Site: _____

URL: _____

Name of Site: _____

URL: _____